CHARLIE'S WAR

Five years ago, Matt broke Charlie's heart and walked out of her life. Now, just as Charlie is about to marry Kent, Matt returns, oblivious to the hurt he caused her. Charlie knows she's doing the right thing in marrying Kent. But Kent has dark secrets that Charlie knows nothing about, secrets which only come to light when tragedy strikes . . .

LINDA GRUCHY

CHARLIE'S WAR

Complete and Unabridged

LINFORD
Leicester

First published in Great Britain in 2011

First Linford Edition
published 2012

British Library CIP Data

Gruchy, Linda.
    Charlie's war. - -
    (Linford romance library)
    1. Love stories.
    2. Large type books.
    I. Title II. Series
    823.9'2–dc23

    ISBN 978–1–4448–1288–6

Published by
F. A. Thorpe (Publishing)
Anstey, Leicestershire

Set by Words & Graphics Ltd.
Anstey, Leicestershire
Printed and bound in Great Britain by
T. J. International Ltd., Padstow, Cornwall

This book is printed on acid-free paper

1

Charlie looked up from the novel she was deeply engrossed in as the train pulled into the station. The sign said Pandleford; two stops more, then. She tucked her legs in as several people disembarked, and the carriage was left feeling echoingly empty. She was vaguely aware of someone settling into the seat behind her as the train started off, but her book held most of her attention.

'Hi, Mum,' came a man's voice. 'On the train now. Should be home in about twenty, thirty minutes . . . okay . . . byeeee.'

Charlie's stomach did a complete somersault. 'I'd know that voice any-where,' she said, standing up. 'Matt.'

Matt stood up and looked at her across the seat back, mouth agape. 'Charlie! Stone me; Charlie Ainsworth!'

1

He neatly stepped round the seat as Charlie turned. They grabbed each other, hugged, kissed cheeks. Charlie felt the shock of his warmth on her, a jolt that left her gasping.

'What are you doing here?' they both said at once.

Charlie sat down, partly because her legs had gone wobbly. 'You first . . . ' she said.

'No, ladies first.'

'I've been visiting my Aunty Sophie in London. Now you . . . '

'I work in Pandleford now. I've been working late on a project; I usually catch a much earlier train. I'm still living with Mum and Dad in Kindleby. House prices, you know . . . '

'You did your degree in computer science then?'

'Yep, got a 2.1 and straight into a job.' Matt seemed justifiably smug. 'What about you? Did you join the army like you were going to?'

'No.' Charlie stood and walked up the carriage. It was empty except for a rough-looking bloke dozing at the far end. She sat back down opposite Matt, and leaned in closer. Her hands were clasped together, resting on her knees, just as Matt's were resting on his. As she leaned in they almost touched; almost, but not quite. She could feel the warmth of his hands close to hers, and it unnerved her.

'No. I joined the police as soon as I could after I left school. I was lucky.'

'Blimey, why so furtive about it?'

'I don't want people earwigging in on our private conversation, that's all.'

'Being a copper's made you paranoid. I thought you were dead keen on the army. You never told me when we . . . in fact . . . ' Matt had a puzzled look on his face.

'Not paranoid, just careful. I don't like yelling my profession down a railway carriage. You never know who might be listening.'

The train speeded up and the noise was momentarily louder as they rushed through a cutting.

'Sorry. So what's been happening over the last few years? You like the police?'

'I love it. I've been a response officer since I started but I've just joined a CID team at Pandleford. Fraud, mainly.'

'You always were good at maths.'

'Like you.' Charlie felt the energy around them rising, as if they were alone, having an intimate dinner. 'I'm living with Mum and Dad for the moment. Saving money.'

'Did you ever hear from Kent Henley? I lost touch with him. Remember when we were at school everyone called us the Three Musketeers?'

'I'm going to marry him.'

Matt could not have looked more stunned if she'd hit him. He flopped back in his seat and looked winded. 'Congratulations,' he squeaked out. 'When?'

'End of the month. When he's back from Iraq.'

'So Kent joined the army, then?'

Charlie nodded. 'We all said we

would when we were cadets at school, but he was the only one who did.'

'But he took five years to pop the question?'

Matt sounded disapproving, critical, and Charlie found herself frowning. 'It's not easy finding the time to be together when you work long shifts like I do and he's off on tours of duty.'

'I didn't mean to sound . . . oh, never mind. It's all a bit . . . ' Matt floundered helplessly. 'Oh, here's my stop. Maybe I'll see you . . . ' The train slid to a halt, and Matt had to get out.

Charlie saw him looking at her though the window, his face forlorn. He raised a hand in a half-hearted wave as the train started from the station. Charlie waved in return, a sad little wave. Slowly the night swallowed him up and the last she saw of him was his pale face and his lovely, unruly dark hair.

As the dark trees and moonlit fields slid by, Charlie's book lay ignored on the seat beside her. Her thoughts were running amok; memories, regrets, pain, flicking through her mind like photographs in an album.

Matt at school, competing with her for top of the maths class; Matt like a caterpillar in his green sleeping bag on Easter Camp; Kent laughing with them both on Summer Camp with the other cadets, old boots buffed into a mirror-like shine. Down the pub once they were old enough, sharing half a pint of cider between the three of them; all pals together, nothing romantic about it.

They'd been inseparable until things started to get serious between Matt and herself. The three of them had still done things together, but the magic of companionship had gone. Then 'A' Levels and plans for the future. Then . . .

Charlie put a hand to her cheek where Matt had greeted her. It tingled still. Such a brief encounter, so little said, so many questions unanswered; like why, when she and Matt had been going out for so long she thought it was a matter of time before he proposed, had he suddenly broken off, shunned her without a word, without any reason, hurting her so badly?

Charlie picked over the memories of her increasingly frantic phone calls to Matt's mobile, messages left unanswered, her emails blocked, Matt's mother's hostility when she'd phoned his home, until Charlie knew it was over between them, she didn't know why, and only Kent was left. Good, loyal, heroic Kent. Her fiancé now.

And here was another question she found impossible to answer — Matt had hurt her so badly five years ago, yet just now their instinct, both of them, had been to greet each other with a hug and kiss. It was only when they had sat down again that Charlie had remembered.

And Matt? Matt had seemed oblivious to how badly he'd wounded her just before he went to university. Why?

It was dark when Charlie got off the train, the night was soft and warm around her. The day had been an Indian Summer day, though Aunty Sophie and she hadn't really benefited as they'd been shopping for Charlie's trousseau.

Aunty Sophie was great at shopping for exactly the right outfit, which was just as well because Charlie soon lost patience and was liable to grab the first thing that fitted. She was an awkward shape, too; tall and broad-shouldered, but slender. Clothes looked good on her but they needed careful selection or they just hung wrongly.

She had a couple of carrier bags of well-considered new clothes to go away in; a gift from her beloved aunty. Charlie lugged her bags along the quiet lanes of Tollington Magna. She contemplated phoning her mum and dad and asking them to fetch her because the bags were getting heavy, but she thought the walk would be helpful in sorting her scrambled thoughts.

Matt. Five years since he'd dropped out of her life like a stone. She'd seen him on 'A' Level results day, hugged him and celebrated with him for his results and university place. Everything had been fine then.

Then he'd gone on holiday with his parents.

Then nothing.

It must have been a holiday romance. Maybe he'd even married the girl.

Why did that thought send such a pang through her? He'd dumped her mysteriously, cruelly, yet all that had been forgotten in those initial few moments today when they greeted each other with a kiss, a kiss which had burned her cheek.

Five years down the line, and she was engaged to Kent now; no way should she be thinking of Matt, not now. Not like this.

★   ★   ★

Her Mum had a supper ready when she got home. 'You spoil me,' said Charlie as she tucked into sandwiches and a slice of homemade cake.

'It's nice to have you under our roof again, even if it's just until you get married. How's my sister?' Charlie's mum sat down with her and took one of the sandwiches.

'Aunty Sophie's fine, sends her love of course, and we managed to find some great bargains. I'll show you tomorrow.'

'Oh, good. The lettings agent phoned. They have someone interested in renting your place.'

'Oh, thank goodness. I was beginning to panic.'

'I hope you're doing the right thing, letting it like that. You hear such dreadful tales about tenants.'

'Mum, we've been through this before. I need to rent it out to pay the mortgage. There's no point in me owning an empty house that might attract squatters when I'll be living with Kent in married quarters on the base. It was perfect when I was actually working in Galenbury but now I'll be working in Pandleford and that's where Kent's garrisoned, it makes far more sense for us to live there. I was lucky with that house, even though it was a bit of a wreck when I bought it, and I love it. Good job Dad's a builder. But I need to rent it out, now.'

Her Mum still looked dubious. 'I know it's sensible but you and your father have got that place done up nicely, and I don't want it wrecked for you.'

Charlie conveyed a forkful of cake to her mouth. 'Oh, yum. This is your best ever. New recipe?'

The tactic worked and her mum was distracted away from the tiresome conversation.

* * *

That night sleep eluded Charlie. Everything was set for the wedding. Kent was coming home soon, then they would be married, a weekend token honeymoon away, and a longer, exotic holiday at Christmas when they both had a fortnight's leave booked at the same time; a rarity.

She had managed to hook herself a good CID job at HQ in Pandleford, quite a coup for a newbie only five years in. It was work she was suited to, good at. She counted herself as ridiculously lucky because all her plans with Kent were falling into place; no mean feat when each of them was blown about by the vagaries of war or the exigencies of duty.

Yes, she told herself in bed that night. Everything was just great and 2004 was going to be a wonderful year.

So why did she feel as if she was suddenly out of control, being rushed into a wedding on a tidal wave, unable to stop or change her mind?

'You're just a control freak,' she said to herself as she finally drifted off to sleep.

★ ★ ★

Charlie donned one of her new suits for work on Monday. She had a training course to do before she could be called Detective Constable rather than Police Constable, and then she would be joining her team.

The course was run in the same building where her new team was based; Headquarters, affectionately known as The Big House. She got to know her team a little in the first few days because she went to see them a couple of times after the detectives course finished for the day. They seemed like a great bunch. Her boss, DI Kaye Benton, was middle-aged and kindly.

Five days in and Charlie felt as if her brain had been treated like a football. She was dizzy with all her new knowledge, and excited by it, too.

She felt desperately in need of a long sleep, and Kent's garrison was due home the next day. She was just walking out of police headquarters when she saw a familiar figure leaving by the same door ten yards ahead of her. 'Matt!'

He turned, blanched. 'Hi, Charlie. How's the new job going?'

'Great. Fine. What are you doing here?'

'I work here. I thought I said on the train the other night. Computer forensics. I get the data people think they've deleted from their hard drives.'

'You just said you'd got a job, not where you were working.'

Charlie thought how attractive Matt looked, even nicer than when they were teenagers in love. She suppressed an impulse to stroke that lock of hair from his eyes the way she always did.

'Sorry,' said Matt.

'Don't keep saying sorry. Please. It gets on my nerves.'

'S — oh. Are you catching the 5.45 train, then?'

Charlie's heart was hammering in her ribs. This was awful. Not only was Matt working in the same place as she was, he obviously caught the same train home.

And for some reason he seemed to

have forgotten about the ghastly way he'd dumped her five years before.

'No. I'm doing some late night shopping,' she told him. 'The troops are coming home tomorrow and I want to get Kent a gift to celebrate.' There; she held up Kent as if he were some talisman against evil, though she wasn't sure if it was to repel Matt, or to repel her own wayward thoughts.

Matt smiled, but it didn't reach up to his eyes, which looked sad. 'Yes, of course. Good. See you around, then. Hope you find something nice. When's the big day?'

'Saturday the 25th.' I hope he's not expecting an invite, thought Charlie. That would be a flipping cheek.

'Two weeks, then.' Matt looked as if he was about to say something else, but changed his mind.

Without realising it they had fallen into step, pace matching pace, just as they had all those years ago on hill walks, except now they were walking side by side towards the railway station.

Charlie peeled away and said, 'Bye then,' without even knowing if the shops were open late. She thought they must be, being Friday. For a horrible minute she thought Matt was going to offer to come with her because he hesitated slightly before continuing on towards the station.

Instead of shopping, Charlie nipped into a cafe and ordered a large latte. She sipped it, vacantly watching people walking past as she tried to arrange her thoughts.

So Matt was actually working in the same building as she was. That meant it would be inevitable that she would bump into him on occasion. So far he'd given her no apology for the appalling way he'd dumped her; he didn't even seem to remember doing it.

She supposed that showed how much she'd grown up in the last five years. Perhaps he was still a callow youth in outlook, heedless of another's hurt. But, thinking back, he'd never been so heedless when they were younger

— one reason why his perplexing behaviour had hurt so much, she reasoned. He'd been the one to notice if she was out-of-sorts, the one to buy her a bar of chocolate when she was feeling down. Not Kent. Kent was protective and manly, but not so sensitive.

Kent now had a fabulous body, well muscled from exercise and training, whereas Matt still looked a bit skinny, really, as if his growth had outstripped his appetite. Well, soon she would be married to Kent and that would be that. It would serve Matt right if he now regretted dumping her. Perhaps that's why he kept looking as if he wanted to say something.

She was doing the right thing, marrying Kent. He loved her. And she loved him. She must do because she'd managed not to give Matt a single thought for at least two years.

Took him long enough to pop the question, she recalled Matt sneering yesterday. Not true. Kent had asked her a few months after Matt had dumped her, but she'd said no, they were too young. She'd said no several times, until one day she thought she might as well say yes because they seemed to spend all their time together anyway.

She drained the latte, stood and went shopping, unsure what to buy. In the end she bought loads of sweets and chocolate because it was too hot to eat chocolate in Iraq and she knew Kent would crave it when he came home. Tomorrow. Her heart swelled and she shivered with anticipation.

2

So many people. So many joyful faces anticipating the regiment's arrival. Girlfriends, wives, kids, relieved mothers, proud fathers; all excited, just as Charlie was. They were all standing in the base, by the parade ground, waiting for them. The emotion was a palpable thing, and Charlie felt herself buffeted by it as she waited.

Somewhere, someone said, 'The coaches have arrived.' The news spread like flames over newspaper. Everyone craned their necks, but nothing happened for long minutes.

Charlie's body was one single ache of longing. She heard the regimental band start up and the regiment marched into the parade ground to the martial music. They looked amazing. There was a collective intake of breath. Her eyes ranged over the men and women until she found Kent. Their eyes locked and everyone else was forgotten.

As a single entity the troops broke ranks, rushing over to their loved ones. The noise of it all ran through Charlie like a shockwave and suddenly she was in Kent's arms, hugging him; crying over him, incoherent with joy and relief. His hungry lips found hers and they kissed shamelessly until she felt her legs go weak.

'Let's go,' Kent said huskily. 'I want to see our home-to-be. I'm shattered and I need a looooong rest.'

'I've got it all ready for us. I started the rent on the first of September. You'll love it.'

The news spilled out of her as they walked along, but she realised after a while that he wasn't really listening. Now that the initial euphoria had evaporated he seemed subdued some-how; tired, she guessed.

The married quarters were laid out on a grid pattern and looked alike except for the colour of the front doors and the state of the front garden. All the gardens were open plan and neat, as behoved a disciplined establishment, but some were more imaginatively planted than others.

Charlie found their house mainly by recognising her car on the drive, and opened the door, leading Kent into their future home. She'd worked hard over the last couple of weeks, moving her favourite pieces of furniture from her house at Galenbury, buying a new three-piece suite, curtains, a really good bed, everything. Kent walked round the place looking bemused.

'Say something, then,' prompted Charlie.

'Like what?'

'Like how much you like it. Like how much you appreciate the effort I've been to.'

'Yeah, very nice. Is the hot water on? I need a bath. And bring me up a coffee, please, love.'

'Okay, It's upstairs on the — '

'I can find a bathroom without being told, don't you think?'

He's just tired, Charlie told herself as she made some coffee. *It's been a long six months. I expect he's feeling a bit . . . shell-shocked.* The word was a little too apposite and she shied away from further thought.

Upstairs Kent was deep in bubbles, body tanned, blonde hair bleached even blonder.

'Thanks,' he grunted shortly as she put the mug on the edge of the bath.

'Shall I scrub your back for you?'

'Ooh, yes, please.'

Charlie scrubbed the loofah over his well-defined muscles, deliciously naughty thoughts coursing through her body, despite the fact they'd decided to wait until after the wedding before living together.

'Oh, that feels so good,' said Kent. 'You have no idea . . . ' He fell silent and his muscles suddenly tensed. He leaned back, a dribble of water sloshing over the edge. 'Thanks.'

Charlie recognised it as a dull dismissal.

She went downstairs, feeling disorientated by Kent's indifference. She sipped her own coffee, idly flicking through a magazine, thoughts still in turmoil.

They had decided that she would live with her parents until the marriage. She wanted the marriage to mean something, not just be a ceremony to get over and done with in between living together. Kent had agreed, though there were times, like now, seeing the suds slide seductively over Kent's back, that Charlie wondered, why wait? Waiting was a bit old-fashioned, though it pleased her parents who had traditional views on the subject. People didn't wait nowadays, so why should she? The wedding was only two weeks away, though. Surely she could wait that long. A delicious thrill of anticipation coursed through her. Waiting would make it better; waiting would make it special.

She heard the water gushing down the drains and movement upstairs into the bedroom. Then silence.

She went upstairs. Kent was sprawled out on the bed in his dressing gown, soundly asleep.

* * *

On Sunday morning, when Charlie's parents had gone to church, she picked up the phone and dialled. 'Aunty Sophie, have you got time for a chat?'

'Cold feet, darling?'

'How did you know?'

Charlie heard Sophie's good-humoured chuckle. 'Educated guess. Now spill . . . '

So Charlie told Sophie about meeting Matt on the train and how it had stirred up all her emotions. Then she told her about Kent's indifference.

'He seemed really pleased to see me at first,' she wailed. 'But then he fell asleep. And when he woke up he was grumpy, didn't want to go out for a meal or anything, so I cooked us an omelette and salad, and just came back to Mum and Dad's.

'I don't know if he still loves me, and I can't talk to Mum about this, I just can't. She's so excited about the wedding.'

There was a sympathetic sigh over the phone. 'First up, love, remember that Kent's been away on active service in a very dangerous part of the world — so dangerous some of them didn't make it back, did they?'

'That's true.'

'And he's just had an exhausting journey, too, love. When you're on edge all the time, living on your nerves, as soldiers at war must, then suddenly the danger goes, it takes a bit of adjusting. I'm not surprised he slept. And I'm not surprised he was a bit indifferent about all the décor and so on. He's probably too tired to take it all in, let alone be enthusiastic. I'm sure he does appreciate it, really. Give him time, love.

'As for this Matt,' Aunty Sophie

continued. 'I take it this is the chap you kept phoning me up about just after you left school, breaking your heart over? And this is the first contact you've had with him for five years?'

'Yes, and yes,' Charlie answered.

'You were in love with him then, but darling, that was five years ago — you were impressionable teenagers, and the way he treated you was abominable. All those feelings he's stirred up now are over a boy who no longer exists. He's grown up now, and so have you. You're remembering your love as a memory. If you hadn't happened to bump into him, you'd still marry Kent, wouldn't you?'

'Yes. Yes, of course I would.'

'So what's changed? Nothing. Just because you bump into an old flame doesn't mean the new one suddenly doesn't burn so hot. Forget Matt, love. He showed his true colours five years ago. He's no good for you, but Kent is. He's been your best pal for years, and now you're marrying your best pal, and

I can't think of a better way to start married life.'

'Thanks, Aunty Sophie. You're right.' Charlie sank back into the sofa, breathing a sigh of relief. She could rely on her Aunty Sophie's common sense.

'See you at the wedding, then. Any time you want to talk, just phone. And cold feet are normal, love, so stop fretting.'

★   ★   ★

'I think you've lost weight over the last couple of weeks,' Charlie's Mum said as she zipped up the wedding dress.

Charlie looked in the mirror. Her reflection smiled back and she looked wonderful.

'Just as well because your wedding dress was a tiny bit tight on me, but now it feels fine. I'm amazed it suits me since I'm normally so hard to find dresses for. I must take after you.'

'I had to put extra lace on the bottom to lengthen it, but apart from that it fits just fine. I remember when I married your dad,' her Mum said wistfully. 'I was terrified I'd put weight on and would burst out of the dress in the church. You look stunning. You've no idea how good it makes me feel to think you're using the same dress. Daddy and I have had a wonderful life together and I hope you and Kent have the same. I've always liked him, such a nice boy, so steadfast, and now one of our brave lads. I'm so proud of you both.'

'Are Emily and Ashley ready yet?' Charlie called to Aunty Sophie, who was dressing her cousins, the brides-maids, in her parents' bedroom

'Nearly,' yelled Aunty Sophie. 'If only they'd sit still long enough to do their hair. And if I hear, 'All right, all right, whatever,' one more time I shall slosh someone!'

The twins were sixteen, and looked very elegant in their long dresses, which Charlie's Mum said would do them for the school prom as well as the wedding.

The photographer wanted to take a

few pictures in the garden before they left, then Charlie seated herself carefully in the stretch limo next to her father.

The limo was Kent's idea, which Charlie thought rather extravagant — if glamorous — because the church was just round the corner from her parents' house. Her parents were regular churchgoers or Charlie might have been tempted to use a Registry Office. But when they approached the church, she was suddenly glad it was to be a church wedding.

She felt very special as she hooked her arm in her father's and they walked up the aisle. Lots of people had come; her friends from work, her new boss, Detective Inspector Kaye Benton, her new sergeant, a couple of pals from schooldays, and Kent's family flown over from the States where his father was now working.

The church was full of young men and women in uniform, the flowers were stunning, the sun was shining and Charlie felt amazing. As she walked up the aisle a movement caught her eye. She didn't look properly, just slid her eyes in that direction.

Matt. Her heart flipped and she stumbled slightly.

Kent looked over his shoulder and gave her a coy look. His best man, Trevor, gave her a diffident smile. He looked startlingly like Kent with his short hair and rugged good looks, but didn't have the same smile.

'Dearly beloved, we have come together in the presence of God . . . ' the vicar started.

As he intoned the ceremony, Charlie had a terrible urge to shout, *Stop! It's all been a terrible mistake!* But she told herself it was just nerves, the same sort of stupid impulse you get when standing on a high cliff.

' . . . Do you, Charlotte Rachel Ainsworth, take Kent Robert Henley to be your lawful wedded husband . . . '

Say no, the little voice told her, *say no.*

But she said, 'I do.'

When they came out from signing the register Charlie got a better look at Matt, even though he was skulking right at the back behind a pillar. He stood quietly and slipped out as she watched him, his expression bleak.

Serves him right, thought Charlie. What did he hope to achieve coming here? Maybe he'd been planning on yelling something when the vicar asked about just impediments and, thankfully, had bottled out of it.

Oh lordy, I shall have to try and avoid him at work, she thought. She could feel her smile stretch into a fixed grin as she and Kent walked down the aisle and out through a guard of honour from Kent's regiment. Then it was time for photographs before being whisked off in the limo to the social club on the base for the reception.

The food was a wonderful buffet; chicken in aspic, quiche, smoked salmon, roast vegetable tartlets, spinach and cream cheese puffs, mini pizzas, sausage rolls, little sandwiches, all washed down with wine, juice, and of course, champagne with the speeches, and the cake.

Charlie was so busy trying to talk to all the guests she almost forgot to enjoy herself. She felt like an actress in her own movie, playing a part rather than really living it.

Kent was in his element, laughing and joking with his friends. Charlie joined him and chatted for a while, but felt slightly excluded by their manly fellowship, so went and gossiped with her mates from her old police station.

She sought out Trevor, the best man, who had just been talking to her new boss, DI Benton. Trevor told her he'd been in the army but had left and now had a job in retail. While Charlie was talking to him she saw that he looked a couple of years older than Kent, was broader of face, but made along the same sort of lines. He could have been Kent's elder brother.

'Time to get changed,' said Kent, suddenly appearing at her elbow. They slipped into a side room and changed into their going-away outfits. Charlie watched Kent shrug into his casual shirt and jeans, loving the way he moved. She wore trousers and a top. The honeymoon was only going to be a couple of days in Paris, arriving home Monday night because she was doing her detective's training. Even a day off had been frowned upon. Their real honeymoon was booked at Christmas. Two weeks in Thailand, and worth the wait, she thought.

★   ★   ★

A constant rumble of distant Parisian traffic was keeping Charlie awake. Kent was soundly asleep beside her, breath soughing near-silently over his teeth. She wondered how come he could sleep so easily and so soundly when it was so noisy.

She stared at the ceiling. They were man and wife now, in fact as well as from the ceremony, but for a time

Charlie had wondered if Kent would let her down in the bodily worship way.

Perhaps the last six months still lay like a shadow over him. *Things will get better*, she told herself. *Look at that fab, fit body in the bed next to you.* She could feel the warmth of that body, glowing with health and vitality. She glanced across at him in the gloom. He really was the most wonderful creature, just enough muscle to look seriously manly without looking grotesque, short blonde hair demanding to have fingers run through it, lips perfect for kissing, cheeks just beginning to roughen with a virile stubble.

She sighed contentedly and laid a hand gently on his chest.

He sat bolt upright and yelled, 'No!' Then he looked round wildly, saw her and groaned. 'Sorry, love . . . bad dream . . . '

He flopped back onto the pillows. Soon she heard his breathing become regular, but she knew he wasn't asleep because in the gloom she could see reflected light gleaming on the whites of his eyes.

She snuggled up to him, tickling his chest until he was properly awake. This time it was better, but still not as wonderful as she'd imagined it would be. *Maybe it needs practice to be good,* she thought. *Perhaps it's foolish to think it's something you can just do by instinct.*

After an early breakfast they went to the Eiffel Tower and paid to take the lift to the top. The views were stupendous. Charlie busied herself with the camera, and a kindly man took a photograph of both of them. Charlie, being a copper, had been ever-so-slightly wary of giving the man her camera, but he hadn't made off with it, and the photo he took was lovely.

They went to Notre Dame in the afternoon, then for a walk along the Seine in the evening before having a meal in a café bistro and watching chic people walking past.

The next day they took a boat trip on

the Seine before taking the train home. 'That was wonderful,' Charlie said as the taxi dropped them off at the front door.

'Wait,' said Kent. He picked her up and carried her across the threshold. 'You've no idea how long I've wanted to do that.'

He kissed her in the hallway, and Charlie knew everything was going to be all right.

★ ★ ★

It was a mile from the house on their base to the police headquarters so Charlie decided she would walk daily. The exercise would keep her fit, and besides, parking at The Big House was very tight. The fresh air revived her a little but her eyes were still smarting from lack of sleep when she got there an hour early, hoping to catch up with the previous day's lessons

Soon she was focused on the course and enjoying herself.

At lunchtime it was a toss-up between the canteen and going into town for a bite. She opted for the canteen and was just tucking into a very unhealthy but very tasty burger and chips when she became aware of someone standing behind her. She turned, expecting to see a companion from her course.

Matt was there, a diffident look on his face. 'Do you mind if I sit down? I'd really like to talk.'

'I'm not sure that's a good idea.'

'But why, Charlie? I don't understand why not, especially now you're married . . . makes you sort of safe, beyond my reach. You weren't so stand-offish on the train, not at first.'

'That's because I'd momentarily forgotten the hurt you caused me,' Charlie replied sharply.

'*I* caused *you*? You're joking!'

'Well that just about says it all, don't you think? If you don't see that dumping someone without so much as a word is hurtful and . . . and just plain wrong. Now will you go away, please? I don't want to make a scene.' Charlie speared a chip and conveyed it to her mouth, though she had suddenly lost her appetite.

Matt sat down next to her as if his legs had stopped working, his mouth gaping. 'As I remember it, *you* dumped *me*. Out of the blue. Told me you wanted nothing more to do with me and it broke my heart. I couldn't understand why, but I did as you asked and blocked you from Messenger and Facebook, blocked your emails. Had nothing more to do with you.'

'I think you'll find your memory's at fault,' said Charlie coldly. 'Now if you'll excuse me . . . ' She stood picked up her tray and started to walked off.

'You emailed me, told me there was someone new and to leave you alone, that you never wanted to speak to me again.' Matt stood up and walked after her.

She turned and fended him off with the tray between them. 'I never sent any such email. You're just using that as an excuse because of the way you treated me.'

'I only did as you asked me to. Left you completely alone.'

'And broke my heart in the process.' She shoved the tray on the rack and stomped off, hoping Matt would take the hint, but instead he pursued her. Several people were watching them quite openly. 'Stop embarrassing me,' she hissed at him.

'Seriously, Charlie — did you really not send those emails?'

'No!' She stopped, turned to look into his eyes. They were full of desperate appeal and for the first time her conviction wavered. 'Are you sure they were from me?'

'Yes . . . at least . . . I was at the time. I was just so stunned I couldn't think straight. You said something like, 'Dear Matt, I've had enough of you and I want to end it. Please leave me alone and never contact me again,' and something else I can't remember. And signed 'C'.

'So I emailed back and asked why, and you said there was someone else, someone better-looking — and richer, that really hurt — and you called me a loser.

'So I sent back an email saying, 'Is it Kent?' but you never replied. I asked Kent but he said he didn't know anything about it. I was devastated when I went to uni. I lost touch with Kent, and, well . . . ' He shrugged. 'And here we are, you're married to Kent and I'm . . . well, I guess I'm a loser after all.'

Charlie chewed on his words as they walked along the corridor. 'Do you still have those emails?' she finally asked.

'No. I deleted them just like I deleted you from my life. I was angry, hurt.'

'Can't you get them back off your hard drive, like you said?'

'Not that sort, no. They're not stored on the hard drive. Besides, I have a new computer now and the old hard drive is in landfill somewhere, smashed to bits.'

'It must have been a mistake,

somehow,' Charlie mused, desperately trying to work out how this had happened. 'You must have got someone else's emails in error and it was just coincidence about the names Matt and C.'

A host of might-have-beens swarmed thought Charlie's mind, but she told Matt, 'Whatever happened, it's too late now. Five years too late, and now I'm married to Kent — and I love him.'

'That's what makes it so hard,' Matt said. 'He was such a good friend and I always liked him. I hope you'll be happy together, really. I'll try and keep out of your way around here. That shouldn't be so difficult, not really. But if you ever need a friend — no strings, just a friend — you know where I live. I mean that, Charlie.'

With that he abruptly turned on his heel and walked rapidly away from her.

★ ★ ★

'What's up, love?' Kent asked Charlie that evening after supper. The plates

41

were stacked up in the kitchen demanding attention but she felt as if she was welded to the sofa. Besides, it was comfortable in Kent's arms.

'Nothing,' she said. 'Just tired. It's quite intensive, this course.' Charlie couldn't tell Kent how she'd been turning today's conversation with Matt over and over in her mind all day long. No way did she feel able to even mention him, but the news of the weird emails kept poking at her subconscious.

'Early night?' Kent said rakishly.

'Good idea,' she smiled. 'Best wash up first though.'

'I meant now.'

'It won't take five minutes, really.'

'Now, woman!' Kent said, laughing as he pulled her upstairs.

3

After Charlie's first week with the team, her new boss, DI Benton asked, 'How are you settling in?' They were having a coffee after wrapping up for the day.

'I love it, it's really interesting. I miss the excitement of Response, of course, but dealing with drunks and domestics gets a bit demoralising after a while. It just seems weird driving a desk. I'm glad I walk from the base or I could see myself getting quite porky.'

'DS Singh is pleased with the way you're settling in — thinks you'll be a great asset to the team.'

'Oh, thanks. That's good to know. I've a lot to learn . . . '

'And how's married life treating you? You always seem to have a smile on your face.' Her boss laughed. 'Sorry. I didn't mean this to sound like an inquisition.'

'It's good. Great. I'm loving it,' Charlie replied cagily.

'But . . . ?' Charlie gave her boss a quizzical look. 'Charlie, I'm a detective, have been for years. Something's bugging you.'

'No, Ma'am, really. I'm just getting used to all the upheavals . . . married, new role, new home . . . and Kent; he's still tired after Iraq.'

'Tired?' DI Benton raised one eyebrow.

'Um . . . sleeps a lot, doesn't like mornings.'

'I've found that men often don't,' quipped her boss.

As she walked home later that day Charlie played the conversation with DI Benton over and over. Something *was* niggling her — but she didn't know what. Something in her subconscious, perhaps. Maybe it was just a residual ghost of regret about what might have been if Matt hadn't received those strange emails. But nothing could change the fact that she was married to

Kent, loved him, had vowed to spend the rest of her life with him. By the time she got home she was happy again.

Kent was already home, sitting in the living room, TV on low, but he didn't seem to be watching it. He was staring into the middle distance.

'Hi there, I'm home,' Charlie said brightly. 'And a weekend off, too. What shall we do? Go out somewhere? Meal? Movie?'

Kent shrugged. 'Whatever.'

'What's wrong, love?' Charlie sat down next to him and wrapped an arm round him. He shrugged it off, stood and went upstairs. Five minutes later she heard him taking a shower.

A little later he came down looking a bit sheepish. 'Sorry love, I'm just a bit tired, that's all. A meal out would be great.' He suddenly froze, looked up as a car drove past, then relaxed just as suddenly. 'Tomorrow maybe . . . I'm too tired tonight.'

Charlie thought an early night would

be sensible, and maybe even fun, but Kent stayed up late surfing on his computer. That really annoyed her, considering how he'd said he was too tired to go out, and she fell asleep before he came to bed.

She woke to find him threshing around. She shook him. 'Wake up! You're driving me nuts!'

He jerked upright, his breath heaving with a strange noise.

'Wake up, it's only a dream,' Charlie reassured him.

He sagged, shuddered, then turned and hugged her.

A little later Charlie knew it hadn't been a wasted early night.

The next morning she found him sorting through the post. He pulled out a couple of letters, handed the rest to her, then locked himself in the loo.

Charlie shook her head in bemusement and opened a lovely letter from Aunty Sophie.

* ★ ★

'I have to work late tonight,' Charlie told Kent a couple of weeks later. 'I'm to help sort out a hang-over job from the last role; a big stolen goods raid I was involved in. It's going to Crown Court soon, so I might be a little busy in the early New Year.'

'It had better not interfere with our holiday in Thailand.'

'It won't. We all fill in forms to say when we're not available. It takes a lot of preparation to find a date when everyone's free; hence the late night tonight.'

'Oh, okay . . . In that case, I'll go out with some mates. They've been pulling my leg about being married and boring.' Kent winked and gave her a hug.

'I'm not sure I like that . . . boring indeed. See you, love.' Charlie kissed Kent, then drove to her old station.

As predicted, it was a long day and she got back to a house in darkness. Kent was still out. She was too tired to cook properly and just ate some toast whilst downloading her emails. She had a laptop while Kent had his own computer; the latest top-of-the-range model with loads of memory. She'd been mildly put out to see he had it password protected, but had decided it was sensible and did the same to hers, though she'd told him her password.

She found herself nodding asleep over her computer, so she went to bed, leaving the landing light on. In the small hours she jerked awake and groped gently beside her to see if Kent was back. He wasn't in bed. Maybe he'd woken her when he came in and was downstairs.

She threw the quilt back, went to the top of the stairs and called out, 'Hi there.'

Nothing. She went downstairs. No Kent. Whatever had woken her, it wasn't him coming home. Wherever could he be? She sent him a text and went back to bed.

She had barely dropped off to sleep when her phone went. It was Kent, sounding very sheepish and very drunk. 'I've been nicked for D&D . . . Sorry, love.'

'You fool,' she snapped. 'How could you do this to me?'

'I know, love . . . I'm truly sorry.'

Charlie spent the night fretting over him. He'd be safe enough in custody, but having her husband arrested for being drunk and disorderly would reflect badly on her and could even affect her career, a career she loved.

Early next morning, Saturday, Kent was home, smelling bad and looking dishevelled. 'I was lucky,' he said. 'They've no-further-actioned it, but my CO has been informed, so I can expect a rollicking about it, maybe even time in the glasshouse.'

Charlie sighed. 'You idiot. Have a shower and I'll put the kettle on.'

After his shower Kent went to bed complaining that his head hurt. 'I'm not surprised,' said Charlie dryly. She got into bed with him and stroked his back idly until he drifted off to sleep.

She stayed awake, despite her disturbed night, looking into the middle distance and letting her thoughts roam.

Later Charlie suggested a walk in the woods since the leaves were spectacular that autumn. The air was fresh with a slight chill to it, the leaves catching the low sun. They seemed yellower than usual, golden, and where they fell there was a tapestry of texture and shape. It was lovely walking arm-in-arm with Kent. He seemed to be chilling out until she stepped on a dead stick. It snapped with a loud crack, and Kent jumped, looked round, suddenly tense for several seconds.

★ ★ ★

Charlie shoved her tray into the rack and was leaving the canteen when she saw Matt staring disconsolately at his meal. She had an urge to brush that wayward lock of hair from his eyes as she used to when they'd been an item, but quickly suppressed it, though she couldn't help sitting next to him.

'You all right?' she asked with genuine concern.

'Fat lot you care. What do you think it's like getting glimpses of you here and there, knowing you're married to another bloke and all because of some accidental emails? I don't suppose you've given one single thought to how I feel about all of this?'

It was true, Charlie told herself. She'd only been thinking of how she felt, and how to protect her marriage from unwelcome yearnings, mainly because she'd originally felt that Matt was the instigator of the entire problem. He'd dumped her without a word, and deserved to reap the consequences.

Except that wasn't what had happened, was it? If Matt was telling the truth about the emails he was just as much a victim as she in this chain of consequences.

She said nothing.

'But actually,' continued Matt, 'That's not what's worrying me at the moment.

I don't suppose it matters to you, but my dad was made redundant a couple of months back and he's having difficulty finding another job. It's causing real friction at home.'

'Eek, not good.'

'I'm helping out with the bills, of course. But that almost makes it worse; unmans poor Dad. He needs a job for his own self-respect. It's just such a mess and I don't know what to do.' He frowned at his plate and toyed with his food.

'Muddle through and hope things get better,' Charlie suggested. As she said it she thought this was an answer to her own problems too — problems she had hardly dared acknowledge existed.

★ ★ ★

Charlie flinched guiltily as DI Benton suddenly sat down next to her late that evening.

'I hope you don't mind, Ma'am. I needed to use the Internet for personal use because it's not easy researching this at home. I don't want Kent to see me looking at these sites.'

'Post Traumatic Stress Disorder? For Kent, or you?'

'Kent. He's not the man I thought I was marrying. He's moody and irritable and keeps having nightmares. And he got drunk the other night, seriously drunk — he even got himself nicked in town.' Charlie gave her boss an anxious look, but detected no censure. 'And I found a bottle of whisky in the cupboard, half drunk. I mean, I like a drink, but . . .'

Charlie scrolled down the page. 'I knew he might be a bit battle-weary when he came back from Iraq, but I thought he'd get over it. Loads of lads and lasses go through the same things and Kent's always been tough. He's the last person I would expect to have a breakdown.' She frowned. 'It's not getting better. If anything he's getting worse.'

'Is he okay in the sack?' The question

was blunt but voiced with concern.

Charlie blushed. 'Sometimes . . . usually, but . . . ' She couldn't go on, couldn't talk over personal details with her boss.

It seemed she'd said enough because DI Benton sighed. 'It does look awfully like it. It's very common, in his profession and ours. You can't ignore it or it will get worse. It needs treating.'

'Yes, but he won't talk about it, won't even acknowledge there's a problem. If I broach the subject he gets all narky and I don't want a row about it. That's why I'm looking it up here and not at home. It says here you mustn't force them to talk.'

'True, you can't force the issue. It has to be his decision, partly because everyone has to find their own path to healing, but he will need help.' DI Benton looked pensive.

'You seem to know something about it . . . '

'Oh, I do. I like to keep an eye on my team for the same sort of things. It can strike out of the blue, years later even. A smell, a sound, a vagrant thought. It's like being dogged by a black shadow. I know because I have suffered the same in the past. I found my way, with help. I think Kent needs help, but he has to be the one to want it.'

★　★　★

'I don't believe it,' Charlie raged down the phone at her old boss. 'I filled in the forms correctly, telling the court when I would be unavailable. If they've started the trial immediately in the New Year, then I'll be away when I'm expected in court.'

'It happens,' the other said defensively. 'Exigencies of duty.'

'It's not an exigency, it's a complete mess-up by the CPS, as usual. I don't know why I filled those forms in if nobody is going to take any notice. Can't you get it changed?'

'No, and you are absolutely needed in court on that day since you arrested one of the defendants. The trial can't get by without you. Sorry, Charlie, but that's the way of it.'

'But this holiday's supposed to be our honeymoon because we couldn't go away before,' wailed Charlie, 'and now I'll have to come back early — and will the new flight be paid for, I wonder? Oh, it's not fair!'

'Sorry Charlie, there's nothing I can do, not now. You simply have to be there.'

* * *

'Tell them to stuff it!' Kent yelled when Charlie told him that evening. 'That's our special holiday and they're ruining it!'

'I can't, sweetheart,' Charlie pleaded. 'I have to turn up or I'll be in contempt of court.'

'Tell you what — leave the police! They can't mess you about like this. I mean it — get another job, one that doesn't muck us around like this!'

'Don't be daft, Kent!' Charlie gasped. 'Even if I did leave the police I'd still have to attend court when they say, otherwise I'd be in contempt of court. Besides, I'm not giving up a job I love.' Charlie raked her hands through her hair. 'I'll have to get a flight home on Sunday the second or Monday the third if the trial starts on Tuesday. It's only a few days off the holiday.'

'A few days . . . ? It's practically a week, nearly half the holiday since we were going to stay on until the Saturday. It's flipping outrageous, that's what it is!'

'Well let's cancel the holiday entirely then. Go another time.'

'It's too late to cancel, we'd never get our money back. Besides, I've been wanting to go there for ages. And the way things are I might not get another chance. I might be killed in action, next tour of duty. I nearly was, you know. I'm not chucking up this opportunity just because of some crummy court appearance.' Kent prowled round the living room, stomping and ranting. 'Tell you what, you tell them to stuff it and come with me like we planned, or I go with one of my mates. Trevor likes scuba diving and I need a scuba buddy — he'll jump at the chance.'

'You can't take a mate on our honeymoon instead of me!' Charlie was stunned. 'I'll just come back early.'

'I paid for this holiday, you either come or I go with a mate.'

'I have to be in court, love; there's nothing I can do.'

'So you love your job more than you love me? Right!'

'I love my liberty! You're asking me to face jail for contempt of court — no way!' She was getting angry now and couldn't believe what Kent was suggesting.

'In fact, it's probably best if I don't go on holiday at all. Suppose there was an airport strike and I couldn't get back in time? Go on, then — take Trevor! See if I care!'

Charlie stomped out of the living

room, slammed her feet into her shoes and went for a walk to cool down.

How unreasonable could he be? Couldn't Kent see that she was bound by duty just as much as he was? He was like a big kid having a tantrum.

She pulled out her mobile and phoned up her old boss at home, told him he'd just about wrecked her Christmas and possibly her marriage.

'Don't blame me, blame the CPS,' he said, not unsympathetically. 'You're not the first copper to have your holiday plans wrecked like this, not by a long chalk.'

When she got home, Kent said, 'It's all fixed. Trevor can come and he's paid his share. I've changed the names on the tickets to his; there was a fee, but Trev paid that too — he's rolling in it and he can afford to. Seems like the best solution, actually. We'll have a special holiday another time.'

All at once he looked worn and bleak. 'Sorry I shouted at you. It's just that . . . ' He turned aside and she could see his fists clenching and unclenching. 'It's just that . . . '

'I think you should see someone, Kent. About all this, I mean; the dreams, the headaches, needing so much sleep . . . losing your rag so easily . . . '

Kent replied with a string of swearwords and stomped off to bed early. Charlie decided to leave him to it. Besides, she wasn't tired, not really.

An hour later she took him a coffee. He was reading in bed, some blokes' magazine full of cars and scantily clad women. He thanked her, but carried on reading.

Charlie dozed on the sofa but later sneaked into bed, careful not to disturb Kent, who had fallen asleep, magazine abandoned on the quilt. Even so, a while later he jerked awake, jumped out of bed, paced for a while before sheepishly getting back in bed and cuddling her.

'What are you doing for Christmas?' asked Matt in the canteen as they happened to put their trays in the rack at the same time. Charlie froze over the question. 'Hey, what's the matter?' asked Matt. 'Have I put my foot in it or something?'

Charlie bit her bottom lip because it was trembling. She shook her head dumbly.

'Look, not being funny, Charlie, but I can see I've upset you and I don't know why. If you've got five minutes, come outside or somewhere less public, and tell me. You don't want to start blubbing here.'

Charlie tried to deny she was on the point of tears, but as soon as she opened her mouth she knew he was right. And despite Diversity Awareness, policing was regarded by some roughty-toughty male colleagues as a man's world where weeping girlies had no place. Weeping in The Big House wouldn't do her career any good at all.

She allowed Matt to escort her

outside to a bench on a street, away from the nick, giving her watch a guilty glance as she did so. She had about ten minutes to compose herself. By that time the urge to weep had gone but she owed Matt some sort of explanation, even though she felt disloyal to Kent in telling Matt she would be alone this Christmas.

She told him about the court case and the wrecked holiday. 'And the more I think about it, the more I can understand Kent wanting to go. I think something really bad happened in Iraq, Matt, something he doesn't want to talk about, and it's made him realise how mortal we all are. He wants to grab life while he can. He proposed to me by letter while he was out there . . . '

'Very romantic,' Matt said dryly.

'No, but don't you see? He wrote a long, romantic letter saying he couldn't bear life without us being man and wife, and to please not say no this time because he wanted to make something permanent. I said yes because we'd been drifting along for so long it made sense, especially as I love him.

'This holiday, it means the world to him and he's afraid that he'll never get another chance . . . afraid because of what happened in Iraq.'

She could feel Matt's warmth as he sat near her but not touching. It was as intimate as on the train that time, and she felt her pulse beginning to race. *This is wrong*, she told herself. *No way will I ever betray Kent, but I wish I didn't feel like this.*

'Poor Kent,' said Matt, and he sounded as though he meant it. 'And poor you. Can't you have Christmas with your folks?'

'Normally, yes. But this year they've done as we did, and booked to go away, since I wasn't going to be in the country. Mum, Dad, Aunty Sophie, Uncle Tim and the twins are all going to Tenerife. So nobody's home.'

'Come to us, then,' said Matt impulsively.

'I don't think that would be very

wise, do you? But thanks.'

Matt blushed. 'I hadn't thought of it like that. And Mum's still a bit funny about you. I haven't explained about the emails yet. I asked you as a friend, nothing more. I know you're married now and I'll always respect that.'

Charlie looked into his eyes and saw only truth. 'I know that now,' she said. 'Next to Kent you're my best friend and always have been.'

★ ★ ★

'A word, if you please, DC Ainsworth,' DI Benton said when Charlie entered her team's room. Her boss didn't look particularly cross, but even so, Charlie's heart flipped as she followed DI Benton into her room. 'Shut the door, please.'

Charlie's heart did another somersault as she complied.

DI Benton scrutinised Charlie just long enough for her to feel flustered, then said, 'You realise that the Big House is a hotbed of gossip and rumour, don't you? Who was that young man you were talking to in the canteen and outside today?'

'That's private,' exclaimed Charlie.

'Not when it's on public display, it's not. Sit down Charlie; this isn't a telling-off, it's a few words of friendly advice.'

Charlie sat down as bidden, her face beginning to glow.

'Charlie, I've dealt with an awful lot of people over the years, and while it's not foolproof, I'm a pretty good reader of body language. The Police Service has a far higher rate of divorce than other professions due to the stress of the job and exigencies of duty intruding on home life. Not least a lot of frisky men and women thrown together in what are sometimes highly charged situations. You're barely married, yet I could see there was some spark between you two.

'I'm warning you for your own sake to be careful of the rumour machine and your own emotions. You know there are Regulations against an officer bringing the service into disrepute and in my book that includes any extra-marital shenanigans.

'So I'd appreciate an answer — who is he, and what does he mean to you?'

Charlie opened and closed her mouth in astonishment, swallowed and then explained about Matt.

'It's nobody's business, but we're just work colleagues. There's nothing going on. Oh, this is outrageous!' she finished.

'You've made your choice and married Kent. If I've noticed the way you look at Matt, others will too, and even if your working relationship is totally innocent, you might find specu-lation isn't so kind. You wouldn't want an unfounded rumour to get back to Kent, would you?'

4

A couple of days before Kent was due to leave, Charlie told him, 'You'd better have your Christmas presents early.' He was to fly out on Christmas Eve and wouldn't be back for over two weeks. She felt a maelstrom of emotions — envy, anger, frustration and regret.

Kent smiled. 'Wait until I've brought yours down, and we'll open them together, have an early Christmas.'

Suddenly he pulled her into his arms and sighed. 'Oh, I wish you were coming. It won't be the same without you. I wish I hadn't thrown my teddies out the pram like that and changed the booking to Trevor and me so quickly. You could have come and flown home early, like you said. I was an idiot. Me and my bad temper. I don't know what got into me.'

'Too late now,' Charlie whispered.

'It's just as well, perhaps; having to come home would've spoiled the holiday for both of us. We can go another time and have a proper, special time away. It'll work out for the best, you'll see.

'Anyway, open your presents.'

'You first.' Kent stood, went upstairs and brought down a huge bag full of gifts. Charlie unwrapped them one by one. A gold necklace and pendant, a Gucci handbag and matching shoes, a silk blouse, and a box of expensive chocolates.

'Wow!' she said, every time she pulled the next beautiful gift from its wrapping. *Crumbs*, she thought, *he's spent a fortune on me. Far more than I could afford to spend on him.*

'I love you,' said Kent simply, as she tried the shoes on.

'They fit perfectly — how clever of you! — and they look great.'

Kent placed the chain round her neck. 'You are so beautiful, and you're mine,' he breathed. They kissed and it seemed things might become more intimate, but suddenly Kent broke off. 'Now for my presents . . . '

Charlie had got him a guidebook to Phuket, some sexy swimming trunks, a couple of books by his favourite author, and lastly some cool shades. He took one look at the sunglasses, blanched, then snapped the case shut. 'They're lovely,' he squeaked tightly. 'Just what I need.' He didn't try them on, which hurt Charlie.

Somehow the enchantment of the evening had vanished, and Charlie didn't know why. Perhaps it was because though the sunglasses were designer shades, the rest of the gifts were rather ordinary, but it was all she could afford.

Kent, from a wealthy family, had always been one for designer labels and classy goods, always been one to splash out on gifts. A handbag by Gucci was a pretty spectacular gift. In comparison her gifts to him seemed a little stingy.

★　★　★

Charlie woke. It seemed lighter in the bedroom than her tiredness suggested; moonlight was creeping round the curtains, lighting the room up.

Kent was sitting up in bed, knees bent, his whole body rigid. She could see the silver light outlining the curves of his muscles. His lips were parted, and his breath was steady as he stared into the distance. Not a nightmare, then. But something gleamed on his eyelashes in the moonlight.

She reached across and swept her hand down his back. He was trembling almost imperceptibly. He looked at her and a silver tear trickled down his cheek.

'What's the matter, love?' she asked.

'Simbo used to wear shades like that. He was a bit younger than me, a good pal. We were in the same vehicle and we were attacked and . . . do you really want to hear?'

'Yes. Tell me. I need to know.'

So Kent told her, still looking into the darkness, voice tense but soft as he told her of all his pain and horror and feeling of helplessness and how, when he really needed to be, he wasn't as brave as he thought he was.

In the end he wept openly and Charlie joined him. She knelt, her arms round him, hugging him, rocking him like an injured child until he grew silent.

'You have to get help,' she said. 'You can't go on like this.'

'Yes, I will, I promise, when I get back from Phuket, I promise. I love you, Charlie, I really do.'

★ ★ ★

Charlie drove Trev and Kent to the airport. They were as excited as little boys at Christmas. Trev kept saying how sorry he was she couldn't go, and then saying how excited he was about going.

He told her his parents had died in a car accident fairly recently, leaving him their house and quite well off, but it had all been a terrible shock and he'd had to sort it all out on his own; the funerals and the death duties and so on. He'd left the army and now he was really happy in a sales job. This was the first holiday he'd had in ages because he hadn't felt like going on his own. He didn't have a girlfriend, hadn't been very good company for a while because he'd been a bit under the weather.

Charlie let the torrent of information wash over her as she concentrated on her driving. They got to the drop-off point and she got out of the car, gave Kent a brief hug, then had to drive off. She saw them both waving goodbye in her rear view mirror.

When she got home the house seemed empty and very quiet. She thought she might as well catch up with the domestic chores. She found it hard to do things when Kent was around. He was good at doing his own washing and ironing, but some things, like cleaning out the fridge or cleaning the oven, tended to get overlooked. Besides, when

Kent was around, she'd rather spend time snuggled up to him. Now he was gone she was at a loss as to what to do.

She'd volunteered to work on Christmas Day. Boxing Day she would be having off, though, and she wasn't sure how she was going to fill the time. A good book, that box of chocolates and some wine, perhaps.

★ ★ ★

Boxing Day, Charlie's TV had been on low in the background, just for company, but now she was watching it with growing horror. A massive earthquake under the sea near Aceh had made the Indian Ocean rise up and slam into the coasts of Indonesia, India, Sri Lanka, Thailand . . . and Phuket, where Kent and Trevor were staying.

There wasn't a lot of news available yet, but what was being shown was bad, awful, beyond belief. Thousands had been killed and many more were feared dead.

The phone rang. Charlie grabbed it so hard she almost dropped it in her haste to answer it. 'Hello?' she said breathlessly. 'Kent?' Her heart was hammering in her ribcage.

'Sorry, no, it's Matt. Have you heard anything? Do you know if Kent is okay?'

Charlie tried to get her thudding heart back under control. 'No. I thought . . . ' *Get off the line*, she silently implored. *Kent might be trying to get through.*

'I'm coming over,' said Matt and hung up before she could say anything more.

A short while later the doorbell went, making her jump. It was Matt, not two colleagues about to convey bad news, so she sagged with relief and let him in.

'Oh Matt, it's been awful. I keep seeing the news about the tsunami and nobody seems to know what's going on. I hardly dare go to the loo in case Kent phones. The death toll keeps rising and they say some British are among the dead.'

'I saw it on the news and immediately thought of you and Kent, but didn't like to phone earlier in case it spoiled your Christmas,' Matt said.

'Christmas is already spoiled, and now this . . . Matt, I'm out of my mind with worry.' Charlie flopped onto the sofa and finally burst into tears.

Matt stood in front of her, looking as if he wanted to hug her but didn't dare. 'I'll put the kettle on,' he said, and found his way into the kitchen. Minutes later he was back with a couple of mugs of tea. He passed Charlie a roll of kitchen towel but by that time her tears had stopped.

'Have you phoned his parents?'

'They're in the States. And I didn't like to use the landline because that's the phone Kent would use to contact me.'

'What about your mobile — can you use that?'

'Charging. The battery was flat.'

Matt fished his phone out. 'Use mine,' he offered. 'And hang the expense.'

Charlie took it but her fingers fumbled so badly that Matt took it back and dialled for her.

Kent's father answered the phone. 'It's me,' Charlie said.

'Charlie? Thank God. Have you heard from Kent?'

'No. I was hoping you had . . . '

'Nothing here. I'm trying to get through to him. He's not on the list of known casualties. They think dozens are . . . Look, if I hear anything I'll phone you back, okay?'

She hung up, handed it back to Matt. 'Thanks.'

The landline rang and Charlie snatched it up. 'Hi, Mum. No, no word at all . . . I can't talk long in case he phones . . . bye.'

She looked up at Matt and told him, 'That was Mum phoning from Tenerife. I do wish people wouldn't keep phoning me to see if I have any news.

My boss DI Benton phoned earlier, and Kent's CO . . . he's doing his best to see what he can find out. I need the line free in case Kent's trying to get through.'

'Tell them to phone your mobile. Or email you. Or you'll email them — would Kent email you?'

'He might. I'll go and check.' Shakily Charlie logged on, but there was nothing. 'I wonder if he phoned my parents' house . . . he wouldn't do that, would he?'

'I shouldn't think so. But I can go and check their answer machine, if you like?'

'Yes please, if it's not too much trouble. I'll get the keys. Mind the phone for me.'

An agonisingly long hour later, Matt was back. He shook his head. 'It was a bit of a long shot anyway. I don't suppose there's any news?'

Charlie shook her head and sat down by the phone again. 'I know how they feel, now, those people with missing relatives. I'm Family Liaison Officer-trained and I should know how to cope, but it's different when it's yours. It's looking increasingly bad . . . Oh, Matt — what if Kent's dead?'

She had the TV on low; the News channel was full of images showing the horrifying extent of the devastation. 'I've never heard of Aceh,' whispered Matt.

It didn't seem real, somehow. It was as if she was watching a disaster movie, and still the death toll kept rising.

'Turn it off,' said Matt. 'Stop torturing yourself.'

'I can't,' said Charlie. She could feel herself trembling slightly and couldn't stop the compulsion to keep watching the news footage. 'Every time there's a clip from Phuket on, I'm hoping I'll see him . . . alive.'

'But Charlie, it's the same clips over and over.'

'I know, but they might put something new on if it comes in.'

Matt spent the day as a shadow,

putting food and drink in front of her, though she hardly ate anything.

'I never expected this,' she said numbly. 'All the time he was in Iraq I was afraid I'd get bad news, was sort of braced for it, like all the other wives and mums. But I thought he was safe now . . . and I should have been with him.'

Charlie watched the news with a strange avidness as the death toll rose . . . and rose . . . and rose . . . and still there was no news of Kent.

'He's a survivor,' she kept telling herself. 'He's a soldier. He'll know how to cope.'

Images flickered over the TV screen of the massive wall of filthy water slamming into the coast, surging inland, turning sun-loungers and cars into a maelstrom of destruction. There were interviews with distraught inhabit-ants, whose families had been torn away on the tide.

Charlie had an increasingly clutching sensation in her heart and began to think that the news of Kent was likely to be bad. 'I want to go there,' she told Matt. 'If he's alive, I'll find him.'

'You can't. You'd only add to the chaos. And you're due in court tomorrow. News'll get through sooner or later. Don't . . . '

Charlie thought Matt had been about to say, 'Don't worry,' before realising just how futile and insensitive that would sound. She saw his eyes slide to the TV, caught up with the awful horror of it all, like motorists rubbernecking at a car crash, only worse, much, much worse.

Later Matt said, 'You should go to bed. There's nothing more we can do today. News just isn't getting through. I'll keep watching the TV in case I see him on the news and I'll keep phoning that information number on my mobile, see if I can get through, but you need to rest, Charlie, especially if you're in Court tomorrow.'

'And what about you? You need to sleep too.'

'I'll kip on the sofa.'

'We'll take it in turns to stay awake,' Charlie told him.

★ ★ ★

The next morning Matt answered the doorbell. The woman on the doorstep said, 'DI Benton, I'm taking Charlie into court.'

'Hi, come in. You're expected.' Matt proffered his hand. 'I'm Matt, a friend of Kent and Charlie's. I'm helping out.'

DI Benton nodded, 'Any news yet?'

'No. I'll be manning the phone today while Charlie's away. I don't understand how some people have got news and we haven't. Charlie's through here, in the living room.'

But Charlie wasn't. She'd jumped up at the sound of the doorbell and was standing behind Matt.

DI Benton gave Charlie a hug. 'I'm so sorry. Have you slept at all? Do you think you're up to this?'

'I'm ready. I'm doing this for Kent.'

Charlie braced herself and followed DI Benton out the door. In the car, as she belted herself in, she said, 'It's very kind of you to take me in like this, Ma'am, especially as it's not even your case.'

'And because of that I can take care of you while you're waiting to give evidence. If you get overwrought in the witness box, we'll ask the judge for a break. They'll understand under the circumstances.'

'I think it will be easier once I'm there, Ma'am.'

★ ★ ★

When DI Benton drove her home later that afternoon, Charlie could tell from Matt's face that he'd had news, and that it wasn't good. Her stomach did somersaults and she felt sick.

'Trevor phoned very briefly. He says he's sent an email.' Matt caught Charlie as her legs gave way and took her into the living room to the sofa. DI Benton followed, uninvited.

Charlie sat looking up at Matt, her breathing stilled. It felt as if an hour had slid past, each heartbeat a minute apart.

DI Benton said, 'Spit it out, man. Is it bad news or no news?'

Matt braced his shoulders, though tears started from his eyes. 'Charlie . . . oh, Charlie . . . Kent's dead.'

'Nooooooo!' Charlie curled up on herself. 'I don't believe it!'

'I'm so sorry,' Matt said, feeling useless. 'Trevor said he ID'd the body and Kent had to be put into a mass grave because of the risk of disease. Trevor wants you to tell Kent's family and friends. He says he's sent an email because lots of people needed to phone and they're only allowed a short call. Can you bear to see if you've got one?'

Charlie nodded and Matt logged on for her, clicked on an email sent from Bangkok. Charlie remembered a news item saying that some of the Phuket survivors had been evacuated there by the military.

Dear Charlie,

There's no easy way to tell you this. Kent's dead. I'm so sorry, but there's no doubt. I identified him myself. Everything is so confused. We never realised the extent of the disaster. It's been awful. I'm so sorry. He's buried in a mass grave because there were so many dead that there is a likelihood of disease. I'm okay. Kent's belongings are lost. Can you tell his family and friends?

Trev.

'Who the heck sends news like this by email?' growled out DI Benton. 'And it's a bit abrupt, isn't it?'

'I expect Trev's in shock, and phone calls home seem limited.' Matt tried to rationalise it.

Charlie felt his hand on her shoulder, comforting. 'I want to be alone,' she said.

'I'll arrange compassionate leave,' DI Benton said. Charlie just nodded and went upstairs, cried for what felt like hours.

When she finally couldn't cry any more, it occurred to her how bad-mannered she'd been, not thanking her boss, not thanking Matt. Slipping downstairs, intending to get herself a drink, she heard a murmur of voices and thought it was the telly until she saw it was off. The voices were coming from the kitchen.

' . . . I'll see if I can wrangle it as compassionate leave for you, too. I don't see why you should give up your holiday entitlement like this. I'll say you're an old friend of the family, which is the truth, isn't it?'

'Yes, I suppose it is. We were all at school together. She may not want me around, might want to be alone with her grief, but this might take some sorting out, and . . . ' Matt faltered.

'So, this phone call from Trevor — what happened?'

'I was watching the news and some of the survivors' stories, hoping to see

Kent, you know — bit of a forlorn hope — when the phone went. It was a bad line, I could hardly hear him. He just said, 'Who's that?' sort of suspiciously, and I told him I was just a friend come round to help, and he said, 'It's Trev. Kent's dead. I'll send an email. Take care of Charlie for me.' So I said, 'Where are you? What about Kent's body?' He said Kent was buried in a mass grave. I got cross and said something like, how did we know he was really dead then and what was he thinking of, letting the body be interred like that, and Trev said he didn't have much choice and hung up. That was that.'

'I'm sorry, I think that's a dreadfully callous way to behave, but I suppose that communication has been down and the scale of it all is terrifying. Do you know much about this Trev?' DI Benton asked.

'Nothing at all. I don't even know if he has family to assure he's okay. But that's his problem. I'm more concerned about Charlie,' Matt replied.

'I'll have to go soon, get back to the Big House and sort this out. Meanwhile take care of her, Matt.'

Charlie slipped back upstairs like a wraith. Things just didn't make sense and it was all too much to take in.

A little later Matt brought her up a cup of tea and a biscuit. 'Do you want me to contact Kent's family? And his CO will need to know, too.'

'It's all right, Matt. I'll come down and we'll do it together. It's my duty,' Charlie sighed.

As soon as Kent's CO heard he came over to offer his condolences and reassurances.

★　★　★

The next day Charlie felt a sort of weary tranquillity now that at least she knew the worst of it. Matt was still here, putting food and drink in front of her, going out for supplies, leaving her alone when she needed it, and demanding nothing in return.

She occasionally watched the news with a feeling of numb resignation. Whole villages had been snatched away, then spat back onto the beach like matchwood. People were forlornly putting up posters, hoping for news of loved ones. Children wrenched from their parents, adults seeking their children. Watching the TV didn't seem to make it any more real, and she kept expecting Kent to walk through the front door. Sometimes she felt a hollow where her heart used to be, and the tears would flow unheeded down her cheeks.

'I suppose,' she said to Matt, looking at Kent's computer, 'I suppose I ought to tell his online friends what's happened. His forum friends, things like that. I think he was friends with some people on a Lotus appreciation group. His email list has all his friends on it, including their phone numbers. He hasn't got a hard copy phone book of his friends. And I'll need to look at his online banking, get that sorted out, stuff like that. But I don't know his password, so I don't know what to do.'

'Do you want me to see if I can break into his system?'

'Oh, could you, Matt?'

'Okay, if you're sure — but please don't spread it around that I've done this,' said Matt. 'Are you really sure about this?'

'Yes. I'd have wanted him to do the same for me.'

* * *

Matt was looking at Kent's files. 'I'm into his system, but he's got loads of stuff from yonks ago . . . Didn't he ever tidy this computer up? Good grief, he's even got essays and stuff from school. It's like he's just transferred every file from the year dot every time he's upgraded his computer. Still, at least he backs everything up properly. Where first? Emails?'

'Yes, please. I'll get the phone

numbers and then I suppose I'll have to phone everyone.'

'Look, as it's quite intimate, you do the reading through and I'll act as secretary, note their names, find out which are friends, which are business contacts, and so on,' Matt suggested.

Charlie agreed, scrolling down a list of old emails, opening them to see what they were about, until they had picked out half a dozen names.

'Check out his forums — look under Favourites,' Matt said.

'Oh, there's another email provider stored under Favourites,' said Charlie. She clicked on it and her heart froze. 'Matt . . . take a look at this. I clicked on it and it's gone to my old email addy, the one I had at school.'

'Are you sure?' Matt pulled up a chair so they were both looking at the screen. 'Let me . . . ' he took the mouse from Charlie, brushing her hand accidentally as he did so. The shock of his touch sent shivers through her body.

There were four emails, all dating

from September 1999, two in the outbox, two in the inbox. They exchanged a look and Charlie saw a turmoil of consternation, fear, and puzzlement in Matt's expression.

'Shall we?' he said.

'Yes.'

The first was from CharlieA26@ to Matt's email address. They read it together. Charlie sought Matt's hand and whimpered and he squeezed her hand in return.

It was the first 'Dear John' letter where she had said she wanted to split with him, never speak to him again, and to block her email, messenger, and Facebook. The next email was Matt's reply, full of confusion and bewildered hurt. Then Charlie had apparently sent a reiteration of her decision, even more forcefully, saying there was someone else, someone better looking, and richer and calling Matt a loser; a horribly vicious and wounding email.

The reply from Matt was heartbreakingly brief: *Is it Kent?*

'I don't understand,' Charlie cried and buried her head in Matt's chest. He hugged her for a long time, rocking her gently.

Eventually he said gently, 'Do you still have that old email address of yours?'

Charlie nodded and silently logged into her own computer. 'Oh,' she said, confused. 'It's not the same, not quite. Look . . . ' Her address was CharlieA–26@.

'That's fraud,' she breathed in pained awe. 'Kent must have set up a similar email address and sent that Dear John email to you. Of course you just clicked on Reply, and it came to Kent, not me. I can't believe he'd do something so wicked!'

'But you didn't answer your phone either,' Matt said, slightly wounded. 'I sent texts and phoned but I just got voicemail.'

'My phone had been nicked and I had to get a new one. I had to change numbers and everything.' Charlie felt cold, so cold she shivered. 'I did try phoning you, lots of times, but you never answered. What if it was Kent who nicked my phone? He had plenty of opportunity.'

'I lost my phone at around the same time. I texted you my new phone number, just in case you changed your mind, but when you didn't answer, I guessed you meant what you said.'

Matt fell silent for a minute or two, frowning at the computer screen. 'I have vague recollections of going to the pub with Kent and you the day before I got the emails. If I remember rightly I was about to go on holiday with my folks. That's the last time I remember having my phone. I got a new one when I came back from holiday because I couldn't find the old one.'

Charlie stood abruptly. 'I need some air! I have to get my head round this,' she said and almost flew out of the house.

She walked briskly to the park, thoughts pursuing her like demons. The cheat! The filthy cheat! He'd selfishly and cleverly broken it up between her and Matt and then gone on to be her best buddy, pretending to console and comfort her.

Poor Matt! Kent must have been pretty desperate to play a beastly trick like that. His fraudulent email had worked, leaving him free to go out with her, and yet it had taken her five years to say yes to a wedding. What did that tell her?

It was cold and wet, low clouds like bruised rags against a louring sky. It matched her mood. 'But I loved Kent. I really did. I know I did,' she told herself. The skeletal trees rattled bony fingers in the wind. She shivered, sat down on a damp bench for several minutes, staring into space, but it was too chilly to linger so she stood and turned her feet back towards home.

Matt met her on the doorstep where she fell into his arms and he gave her a long, reassuring hug.

'I loved him, truly, I did. But this

feels like such a betrayal and it hurts, Matt, it really hurts.'

'I know, love.' He kissed the top of her head. 'Of course you loved him, the parts of him you were allowed to see. I saw that on your wedding day. It broke my heart, even though I was happy for you. I thought it was your decision.'

He ushered her in, look her coat from her as if she were a child, made her sit while he made a mug of tea. Her fingers were cold and she was chilled right through, and not just from the temperature outside. Her teeth chattered and the tea felt too hot in her mouth.

'If he hadn't cheated like that, you and I might have been married by now. Things might be very different,' she said.

'Yes, but we can't change the past,' Matt told her softly. 'We just have to learn to live with it.'

★　★　★

Later that evening, after Matt had prepared a light meal that Charlie just picked at, he said, 'If you think you'll be all right on your own tonight, I think it might be best if I don't stay over again. I saw the look in the CO's eyes yesterday. It felt so right when I thought you needed the support, but now it feels wrong to stay overnight. I suspect you need some space anyway, especially now. But I'll come round tomorrow if you need me.'

He laughed sadly. 'Besides, I have to go home — I need a change of clothes.'

'Oh Matt, I never thought,' Charlie said. 'You could have worn some of Kent's.'

'And how would that have made you feel?'

'Still, I should have thought . . . yes, please come round tomorrow. I still have so much sorting out to do. I'll have to have an inquest to get a death certificate without Kent's body, and Trev ought to be called as a witness when he gets back . . . and there's Kent's life insurance to claim on, his bills to settle . . . all sorts. I'm not asking you to do it for me, but it would be nice to have someone around. And I've got other, ordinary worries to sort out, like my house. Apparently the tenants didn't pay the last month's rent and have done a flit. I got a letter from the letting agent this morning . . . just what I need right now.'

'Okay, I'll drive you over there if you like. Tomorrow, then.' Matt stood and kissed her cheek. 'I'll see myself out.'

5

Once he'd gone, Charlie absent-mindedly washed up. What an absolute hero Matt had been the last couple of days . . . helpful, protective, mindful of her feelings . . . but what *were* her feelings? She'd just found out that her dead husband had acted despicably to oust his rival.

Kent used to say, 'All's fair in love and war,' but she didn't think he meant it like that. But she loved him and missed him.

She remembered the way she felt when Matt put his arms around her protectively, and how she had mentally shied away from such feelings as a betrayal to Kent's memory. It felt unseemly, somehow. Maybe Matt felt the same. Maybe that's why he'd decided to go home.

★ ★ ★

Next morning Charlie felt more composed and resigned. She made a list of things she had to do and started doing them one by one. The first thing, she decided, was to phone the life insurance company and explain the situation. It turned out they'd had quite a few devastated relatives phoning up. They asked her to forward on the email from Trev.

Charlie heard the post flop onto the mat, so went to fetch it. There was a condolence card signed by Kent's mates in the regiment and a magazine for Kent, which she put on the side for him as she always did . . . the habitual action made her sob.

She'd best cancel his subscriptions, she reminded to herself. The last envelope was addressed to both of them and she tugged it open and scanned it.

It was a credit card bill. A big one. A staggeringly big one. Where had that come from and why was it in joint names?

Her legs had suddenly gone wobbly again and she sat down at the table as she stared in disbelief at the figures. On the latest statement was the Gucci handbag and some of her other Christmas gifts from Kent, gifts she no longer felt comfortable with now she'd seen this. With any luck, she'd be able to return them. The interest rate was zero for four months but the minimum repayment made her wince.

She felt a surge of blind panic. She didn't have credit cards, didn't believe in them; the only debt she had was her mortgage. She read down the list of what Kent had used the credit card for in the last month. Magazine subscriptions, the changes to the holiday booking, her gifts, new shoes . . . how much? How could he continue to spend when he owed this much? And on fripperies like her gifts and magazine subscriptions.

She remembered his furtive behaviour with the post, grabbing the envelopes and disappearing into the loo, locking the door. This must explain it; he hadn't wanted her to know, unsurprisingly. She logged into Kent's computer and looked at his entire, sorry financial mess.

The doorbell made her jump. Matt was standing on the doorstep with some groceries.

'I suppose you could go to the NAAFI but I thought I might as well get some stuff in for you . . . hey . . . what's wrong?'

Charlie explained what she'd found. 'I can't understand it, Matt. I never asked for a joint credit card. I don't believe in them, and being unable to manage your debts is a disciplinary offence for a copper. I'm really scared now.'

'Was he insured? Could you pay these debts off with his life insurance?' Matt asked.

'Yes, but there's no body, and the only evidence we have of his death is that email, hardly good evidence. I don't know what the insurance company will do, but I'd better not rely on that. Oh, Matt, I might have to sell the house. Perhaps it's just as well the tenants have flitted.' She was cold again, wringing her hands and rocking to and fro.

'Tell you what, let's go out. It's all been too much and I think you need time out. We'll take a look at the house and go for a pub lunch. My treat.'

Charlie's first instinct was to refuse, but perhaps Matt was right and she did need to put her grief and confusion aside for a while. 'I'd feel a bit disloyal to Kent if I do that . . . '

'Disloyal? Why? Because it's me, or because you might be happy for a while? I'm not trying to take advantage of you; I'd never do that with the emotional state you're in, but I do want to make sure you're okay. Come on, we ought to go and see the house at least, and I don't think you're fit to drive.'

Charlie watched the scenery flitting past. It was true Matt was acting more like an elder brother than an old flame just now. It made it easier because, though her mind said looking on Matt as a potential lover was immoral, her body said otherwise.

She began to recall the old times, the good times when they were still at school. He still had the same mannerisms, the same quirky grin, the same sense of humour and sometimes she felt as if the last five years had just been a dream. *Stop it*, she told herself. *He's right. You're far too vulnerable to be falling in love right now.*

'Oh no,' she groaned as they approached the house. She could see an old mattress in the garden and it didn't augur well. The garden was unkempt, the grass like a meadow.

'Nice house,' commented Matt with a slightly envious tone.

'It's an ordinary semi, but solidly built. I bought it at an auction with Dad and we did it up. It was, in estate-agent speak, 'in need of some refurbishment' which basically meant it needed gutting, rewiring, heating putting in, new bathroom, new kitchen, decorating, the lot. Dad helped heaps. I used to live in one room and do it up on rest days. I always thought I was going to live there, but then Kent proposed and it seemed easier to live on the base and rent this out. I didn't want to sell it because I wanted somewhere for us to live if he left the army — but now I might have to, to pay his debts.'

'I'm not sure that's true, love. If you didn't know about the credit card and it's not joint or underwritten by you, I don't think you have to pay them off. It's his debt. Don't pay them off in a panic; get some advice first.'

'I think I have to settle any debts out of his estate, and that will include the credit card debts, I suppose. And what really worries me is that the credit card does look like a joint one, even though I had no knowledge of it. I'm worried I might be responsible for it . . . I'm scared of debt . . . I hate owing.'

'Good job you didn't do a degree then,' said Matt ruefully. 'I have a huge student loan to repay. It's as if I've mortgaged my life to get a degree.'

Charlie slipped the key in the lock. A

shut-up, chilled stuffiness mixed with old food smells hit them.

'I think I'll look in the kitchen first.' Charlie led the way through the hall and into the kitchen, dreading what she would find. It was empty and, though not clean, not as filthy as she feared. A bin liner with a couple of teabags and a mouldering crust of bread explained the smell. Charlie opened the back door, looked out briefly and then closed it. 'They were supposed to maintain the garden. Honestly, how hard would that have been? The grass hasn't been cut in six months.'

'It's a big garden.'

'There's a lawnmower in the shed.' She opened the back door again, went to the shed, and said a rude word when she looked inside. 'They either took it with them or sold it. I suppose I shouldn't be surprised, but I am.'

'Did you let it unfurnished?' asked Matt.

'Part furnished. There was a bed and some ancient bedroom furniture, a dining table, a few odd bits like that. I took the modern bits with me to furnish the house on the base. Kent didn't like old stuff.'

They looked over the house, feet clattering on the laminate flooring. Charlie was glad they'd installed laminate because she had the feeling the carpets would have been filthy by now because the vacuum cleaner she'd left behind was exactly as she'd left it. The curtains were gone, as were some bits of furniture, but the big, heavy stuff was still there.

The bed had been dismantled. 'I've just realised that's my mattress rotting in the garden,' she said. 'I think they tried to nick the bed but it was too much. I'm just not sure what to do now — whether to sell the house, or tidy it up and rent it out again, or move into it and live here again . . . ' Charlie fretted.

'You don't have to make any decisions just yet, do you? See what happens over the life insurance. See a solicitor and talk to the credit card company, find out how come your name's on the account. You need to give yourself a breathing space.'

'I hope I don't get squatters,' she said, locking up carefully.

The pub was warm and welcoming, and the bar menu looked tempting. For the first time since Boxing Day Charlie realised she was hungry. 'I really fancy the steak pie,' she said.

'Me too,' Matt agreed, then, 'No, actually, I think I'll have the lasagne. What'll you drink?'

'Half of bitter, please.'

'I'm driving, so I'll stick with cola.'

They bagged a table by the fire where Charlie began to thaw out. The food was excellent and she felt her nerves unknotting one by one as she stared into the dancing flames, watching the orange flickering over the shimmering red log, the ash falling into the grate in glowing drifts. She could understand how people once thought you could read auguries or see the future in the flames, but if that were possible she was blind to it. To her, the future was one of muddle and confusion with an overlay of grief.

Instinctively she sought Matt's hand and he gave it a reassuring squeeze.

★　★　★

When they got back, Charlie's mum and dad were sitting in their car, parked on her drive. They looked relieved when she got out of Matt's car.

Charlie threw herself at her mum, hugging her, then hugged her dad in turn while Matt looked on.

'Do you remember Matt from school, Mum?' she asked. 'He's been been really amazing, helping out with stuff.'

'Yes,' said her mother with an edge of reserve.

'Em, I think I'll go now, Charlie,' Matt said uncomfortably. 'If you need any help with anything, just yell.'

With a stubborn jut of her chin, Charlie gave Matt a hug. 'Thanks for everything. I'll phone later,' she whispered.

The first thing Charlie did when she got inside was put the kettle on and her mother pursued her into the kitchen.

'Was that the Matt who dumped you without a word? I thought I vaguely recognised him,' she asked angrily. 'What's he doing here? Kent's barely dead and you're out having fun with an old flame — and I can smell beer on your breath. You've been to the pub. How could you?'

Charlie's dad hovered in the doorway, a disapproving scowl darkening his face. 'I never believed any daughter of mine could behave like a tramp.'

'Mum, Dad, stop jumping to conclusions. Matt took me to see the house because the tenants abandoned it and he didn't think I was safe driving. And yes, we had a meal at a pub and I had half a pint with it — it actually made me feel just a tiny bit better.' Charlie was indignant. 'This has hit me harder than you could possibly imagine, and for reasons you don't know about. Matt was the only one who was around and he's been no end of help. I was on my own, out of my mind with worry on Boxing Day, and then, when I found out . . . '

Charlie paused and gave a shudder. 'And there's something else you should know . . . all those years ago Matt got an email supposedly from me, but which I hadn't sent, saying he was dumped and never to contact me again — so he didn't. It was all a ghastly mistake.'

'How could you say marrying Kent was a ghastly mistake?' her mother gasped. 'I always preferred him to Matt. He was more attractive, better dressed, better groomed — '

'Yes, and now I'm going to have to pay for all Kent's grooming and nice clothes,' Charlie interrupted. 'Mum, please don't go on. I don't want to row about Matt. It's not like you think and he's been nothing but a gentleman, like a brother, helping me when I needed it most. There's nothing between us.' As she said this, the last remark sounded like a lie to her. 'Kent left about £20,000 worth of debt. And I'm not sure if I'll have to pay it or not. That's what I meant about paying for his nice clothes.'

Her mother drew a sharp breath. 'No, darling. That's awful!'

'That's only the half of it, but I can't bear to go into the rest of it, not just now. I feel like I'm in my own tsunami, with all sorts of things slamming into me, and you're not helping. You're my parents, I thought you'd come to support me, not have a row about an old friend.'

'You mean Kent came into the marriage with a whole load of debt hanging round his neck? £20,000? That's incredible! His parents ought to pay up!' her dad snarled.

'You mean, hit his grieving parents with a massive bill?'

'Why not . . . you were, and none of this debt is your doing,' said her dad.

'His parents are well-to-do. They could afford it.'

Charlie made tea and they all retreated into the living room.

'Sorry we shouted at you,' her mum said feebly. 'What are you going to do?'

'I'm not sure yet. Everything's still up in the air. I need to find out if I'm responsible or if his debt died with him . . . except he's not legally dead, and every month that slips past will add to the debts because of the interest and the minimum payment's huge. Oh, I'm so confused. I feel like screaming, for all the good that will do.'

'Come home,' her dad urged her. 'We'll take care of you, no need for Matt to put himself out any more, not now we're home.'

'Thanks, Dad but I have loads of things to sort out here, and I'd prefer to be on my own to sort my head out, if you don't mind. And I'm expecting phone calls on this number.'

The thought of being at her parents' house, with Dad treating her as if she

was twelve years old, was suddenly claustrophobic. Her dad looked rebuffed and
she felt guilty.

★   ★   ★

Once they'd left, the choice was either
not watch the TV at all, or put up with
the latest on the disaster. Now there
was fear of disease spreading amongst
the survivors; cholera, typhoid, and
malaria. People were without homes,
without drinking water because of salt
contamination, and without warm
clothing. The rebuilding of the com-
munities would take years, decades.
Forever, maybe.

So many dead, so many still at risk.
The steadfast stoicism of some of the
survivors humbled Charlie, though
sometimes it all felt so unreal, like a
movie she was watching.

She decided to call her Aunty Sophie,
hopefully before her opinion was
tainted with a phone call from her mum
— and poured out the parts of the story

she didn't mind sharing.

'I can understand why they had to bury Kent in a mass grave,' she said over the phone. 'But that adds to the feeling of it not being real. I keep half-expecting Kent to walk in through the front door as if nothing had happened.'

'Uhuh,' Aunty Sophie agreed. 'I felt like that when my mum died. It wasn't until the cremation that I really started to believe it. And even then, months later, I'd read a book and think, 'I must lend this to Mum'.'

'Well, that's just it; I need the sense of closure you get with a funeral, but I won't get that.'

'Certainly not with that Matt around. He's nipped in pretty quick, hasn't he?'

'It's not like that, Aunty Sophie.'

'What's it like then? What's his motivation?'

'He cares, that's all.'

'So it is 'like that'. But that's not necessarily a bad thing, love. If he really cares for you, and you for him, then it might be what you need. Stuff the gossip — but do be careful, Charlie. It's easy to think you're in love with someone when you're vulnerable. And that's what frightens me most.'

★ ★ ★

'How are you?' Matt asked when he phoned the next day.

'I'm worried about being away from the phone, but I suppose people have my mobile . . . I just feel I need to get away for a couple of days . . . '

'Too many memories?' Matt asked.

'Sort of. I had an answer from the insurance company; they said they'll cough up half the amount Kent was insured for as an interim payment, but they won't pay it all until there's been an inquest and a proper death certificate. I wish I knew where Trevor is. Surely he's back by now? I'd expected him to come round, tell me what happened in person.

'Anyway,' Charlie sighed. 'The interim

payment will clear the credit card debt, so at least my house is safe. But he made it a joint card by transferring the debts from one card to another soon after we were married. He forged my signature on the papers to increase the limit. I just can't believe he did that; it's fraud big time. As far as the credit card company is concerned I signed the papers, so I'm responsible.

'No wonder Kent was so furtive about the post. I asked his parents if they could help out and, well, they were a bit hurtful.' Charlie blinked. 'Your debt, your problem,' they said. Yet Kent's family weren't short of a bob or two.

'The letting agent says it's very quiet for lettings at the moment so I don't know how soon I'll get another tenant,' she added. 'I'm going to move the furniture from here to there and try and let it furnished, then stay at Mum and Dad's until I get settled. Not ideal, but . . . '

'How much per month do you want

for it? Let me rent it,' Matt suggested. 'My mum and dad are moving up north — he got offered a job and they sold their house just before Christmas. The completion date's coming up soon and Dad's new firm are paying for relocation. I've been looking all over Pandleford for a place to live. It would help me out and it would help you out.'

'Are you sure?'

'I need somewhere to live, and I can just about afford that. But think about it, don't let me rush you. I'm going back to work tomorrow, but I'll be around in the evenings if you need me.'

* * *

Charlie's dad and Matt worked with each other in frosty silence, loading the furniture from the married quarters house into the back of Charlie's dad's truck. It was an open-backed builder's truck but the weather was dry, so it didn't matter.

'Are you sure you know what you're

doing?' her mother asked for what seemed like the hundredth time. 'Matt might be as bad as your last tenants — worse, he might abuse your friendship and good nature. I bet he has a huge student debt and won't be able to afford the rent.'

'I'd trust him more than I'd trust an unknown, Mum — look how that panned out. I'd rather he rented it than I got squatters in it. Though it's a lovely house, it is rather out-of-the-way and not so easy to rent out as a flat in Pandleford.'

'Are you saying you bought the wrong house, then?'

'No, I love the house! But it's in a village on the wrong side of Pandleford for London, that's all I'm saying.'

'I don't know how you can bear to use the furniture you and Kent bought together . . . '

Charlie thought she would scream in frustration.

'I'm not the one who'll be using it. Anyhow, with the state of my finances, beggars can't be choosers. For good-ness sake, Mum, it's not as if I'm going to be living with Matt. That furniture means nothing to him. Yes, it breaks my heart when I think of those three short months I had with Kent, but . . . '

Suddenly she found herself in tears.

Her mum wrapped her arms round her, rocked her. 'I'm sorry, darling, I'm so sorry. I only asked because I'm worried about you. We want what's best for you, but you're still so young.'

Matt came in and Charlie saw his face drop. He put a comforting hand on her shoulder and walked out again.

A few minutes later he came back with Charlie's dad. 'Nearly loaded up,' her dad said. 'Kent's clothing is in a load of bin bags, what do you want me to do with them?'

'Charity shop,' her mother said immediately.

Matt cleared his throat nervously. 'Actually, it might be better to put some of them on eBay. They're expensive suits and — '

'How could you think my daughter could bear to sort through his clothes and flog them in cold blood?' she snarled at Matt.

'No — but I could . . . '

'You mercenary little toad.'

'Look, I rather think that's Charlie's decision, don't you?' Matt defended himself. 'She's twenty-three, for goodness' sake, not your little girl any more. She can think for herself.'

'Oh, stop fighting,' Charlie cried. 'Mum, Matt has a point. Kent's debts and fraud left me up the creek and any money would be useful. If Matt is kind enough to sort through Kent's stuff and sell it for me, then I really appreciate it. I can't afford to be picky and I know that some of those clothes haven't even been worn.'

6

Matt saw Charlie in the Big House canteen next day, and approached her table, saying, 'Hello, landlord. How's your first day back been so far? Can I sit down?'

'Be my guest,' said Charlie, pulling her dinner tray closer to herself. Matt sat down opposite her and flicked his hair back in the way that melted years and her heart rate soared.

'I'm glad I'm back at work,' she told him. 'I needed the time but now it's time to try to start moving on. I'm trying to remember the best of Kent, the things I loved about him, the good times we had, and forgive the emails and debt. Otherwise every time I think of him it hurts.'

'How's living at home with your parents?'

Charlie frowned. 'It's okay, but Dad

keeps giving me inquisitions over my finances and how I'm coping with Kent's debt, and Mum keeps going on a bit about playing the field.'

Matt laughed. 'I take it she still doesn't approve of me, though it's understandable, I suppose. My mum and dad are moving this weekend. I'm going to miss them but it's nice to have a bit of independence.'

Charlie found herself thinking randomly ... his hands were really exquisite, an artist's fingers but with an underlying strength. She liked the way he held his knife and fork, the way he conveyed food to his mouth ... those lips with that cute quirk.

Stop it! Her thoughts were making it hard to concentrate.

'I'm going up north this weekend to help them unpack.'

'Okay,' she said. The conversation was suddenly bogged down with nowhere to go. Charlie wondered if he was hoping for help from her. They ate in silence until their plates were empty.

'Has a date for Kent's inquest been set?' Matt asked. 'And any word from Trev?'

'Yes, and no. It's really odd, Matt. I can't believe Trev hasn't come to see me. I would in his circumstances. Maybe he feels guilty about Kent or something? Maybe he could have done something to help and can't face me over it?'

'Where does he live? Why don't you go see him?'

'I don't know, but that's a good idea. I'll see if I can find his address in Kent's stuff. Surely he's back by now.'

It was a longer journey than she'd anticipated, about an hour, but she finally found Trev's house; a very nice-looking property with neighbours either side but fields on the other side of the road. Lucky Trev, Charlie thought — or perhaps not so lucky, since he inherited it from his parents.

As it was Saturday morning she hoped he would be in. She'd contemplated phoning ahead, and only the suspicion that Trev was avoiding her prevented her from doing so. There was a car on the drive, which augured well.

She left her own car parked on the road despite the roomy drive, and rang the doorbell. It was answered almost at once by a woman dandling a baby on her hip, which completely flummoxed Charlie for the space of five heartbeats.

'Oh, hello. I'm looking for Trev . . . Trevor Hardwick.'

The woman looked perplexed. 'He's not here any more if he was the last tenant. Moved on. I got some post for him, official looking but didn't know where to send it.'

'Oh. That's a nuisance, I really need to talk to him. Maybe your landlord knows where to find him?'

'I asked but they wouldn't give out anyone's address, said it was confidential. I can take his post round to them and they said they'd send it on to him.' The baby started grizzling. 'Sorry, I can't help you.' The woman closed the door in Charlie's face.

Charlie went back to her car, sat in it, checked the address. Yes, it was the right one, and the woman had said that she had some post for Trev, so it was definitely the right place.

But it didn't make sense. Trev had told her he owned the house, yet the woman implied he was just a tenant. Bother — that meant he could be anywhere.

She went back up the drive and rang the doorbell again.

'What do you want? Are you a debt collector? Go away,' the woman called from behind the closed door. 'He's not here any more. You woke the baby. Go away.'

'Sorry. I'm not a debt collector, I'm a friend of Trev's. I need to see him urgently. You know he was caught in the tsunami?'

'No. How would I know that? I didn't know him.'

'Who's the letting agent, please? Perhaps they can help.'

'Go away or I'm calling the police.'

Charlie felt like saying, *I am the police* in a deep dramatic voice, and the thought made her giggle silently, though she sobered almost instantly.

'Sorry to have troubled you. Can you please get that post for Trev to the Lettings Agent as soon as possible? He's needed for his friend's Inquest. I could take them, if you like. I am a police officer, though this isn't official business. You can trust me.' Charlie reached for her Warrant Card, before realising it was in the pocket of her jacket which was still in the car.

'Go away. I don't care who you are.'

'Can I give you a letter to go with his other mail, please?'

'No — now go away.'

She walked down the drive. Was anything as it seemed? Kent had lied and fraudulently forged her signature, and now it seemed that Trev had lied about owning the house. He'd been a tenant in it and now he'd gone.

Perhaps he owed money — or maybe that was Mrs Trev Hardwick with the baby and he'd lied about being single and unattached. But if so, why?

Maybe her memory was at fault. Or maybe Trev had decided to let the house and he was the landlord. She looked for her jacket in the car. It wasn't there. She must have left it over the back of the chair at home. Bother. She checked her handbag in case her warrant card was in there, knowing full well that it wasn't, but checking just in case. She chided herself for being so careless. On the other hand, it wasn't a good idea to flash her warrant card round like that when it wasn't police business.

She drove to the nearest town, parked and wandered up and down the high street. It was a small market town and all the shops were round a market square. She went to a coffee shop and sat down over a latte.

What a waste of time the journey had been. Maybe she could phone all the local letting agents and see if any of them knew Trev. But they were under no obligation to help her at all. Why should they?

After she finished her coffee she prowled up the high street, and found an estate agent's.

'Excuse me, I hope you can help. I'm looking for a lettings agency,' she said to the middle-aged woman who was seated behind a computer.

The woman looked vaguely disappointed. 'There's one attached to this agency. Upstairs.' She turned back to her screen dismissively.

Is everyone round here rude and unhelpful? Charlie pondered as she clomped up the stairs. She explained her quest to the woman there, who could have been the elder sister of the one downstairs, in looks as well as unhelpfulness.

The woman shook her head. 'Can't help you there,' she said. 'Client confidentiality and all that.'

'Okay, thanks. I understand.'

What a waste of time this was, Charlie thought as she belted up. She sat there thinking. It had been an hour's journey and still she was no nearer to finding Trev. It was entirely possible he wasn't even back from Thailand yet. Maybe he'd stayed behind to help with the clear-up.

The woman with the baby had irked her. Maybe Trev was living at the address after all. Charlie drove back, parked up a little way away. There was a second car on the driveway now. Half an hour later the woman came out of the house, still holding the baby. A man followed holding a baby car seat, which he fixed into the back of the second car. Not Trev, definitely not Trev because this man was black. Charlie hadn't really looked at the baby, but thinking about it, the amber skin and the tight curls indicated that this man was his or her daddy carrying the car seat. So this family was definitely nothing to do with Trev.

Charlie wasn't too hopeful of Trev getting his important mail even if he had left a forwarding address with the lettings agent, at least not in time for the Inquest. The woman had seemed totally disinterested.

Disgruntled, Charlie drove home to her mum and dad's, wrote a letter to Trev at that address and put it in the letterbox with a first class stamp on it. With any luck, the woman would pass it on. Eventually.

* * *

'You're working late.'

Charlie's head shot away from the computer screen and looked round. Matt was leaning on the doorjamb, hair flopped over his eyes.

'You made me jump,' she said. 'I hope the move went well.'

'Yes, ta. And sorry for making you jump. I was just on my way out. It's late, way past home time.'

'I know, but if I stay late it's less time at Mum and Dad's.'

'Getting nagged again?'

'No, not really. It's just that Mum

and Dad do things differently from me. It was okay for a short while when I was living there before my marriage, but now, with no end in sight, it's getting on my nerves, and I've only been there a short time. Little things like the way I fold my tee shirts. Mum unfolds them and folds them up the 'right' way. I should be grateful that she does so much for me and I don't know why that bugs me so much, but it does. I'm a miserable ingrate.' She smiled ruefully.

'Let's go out, then. A pub, or the movies, maybe a night club or something. As pals, of course.'

'Yes,' said Charlie, pushing her chair away from the desk and standing up. 'Let's do that. You are my best pal, after all. But not a nightclub because it reminds me of the drunken idiots I used to nick when I was on Response. A film, maybe.'

'How does *March of the Penguins* sound?' Matt suggested.

'Great, actually. I don't want anything emotionally heavy.'

Side by side with Matt in the cinema, sharing popcorn, Charlie was acutely aware of his body, their legs occasionally touching. She could feel the heat of his firm thigh through his trousers. As she became engrossed in the film it was as if the years had fallen away and they were still teenagers in love.

When the film ended she was startled to find her head leaning on Matt's shoulder, his arm across her shoulders.

He seemed just as shocked because he jerked it away. 'Sorry,' he said awkwardly.

'I'm not,' Charlie replied.

'Really?'

'Kent's dead, Matt, and though I loved him, I loved you before he . . . Why should he still come between us like a ghost? After the way he split us up I don't feel I owe him anything now. I loved him, he's dead, and that's the end of it.'

His arm tightened around her, urged her to turn to face him, she lifted her lips and he kissed them, hesitantly at first, then with passion. A flame spread through her from her head to her toes, and she shivered deliciously.

Outside the cinema, Matt said, 'Let's eat . . . intimate Italian or a cor-blimey kebab? The choice is yours.'

'Kebab, I think. Let's save the Italian for another night.'

As they walked back to the Big House where their cars were parked, tucking into kebabs, Charlie said, 'It'll be spring soon. There's a warmth in the air.'

'Yes. I've cut the grass once already.'

'You found the mower after all, then?'

'No. I bought a new one — and put a hefty lock on the shed.'

'I'm tempted to come home with you tonight and inspect.'

Matt stopped short and looked down at her. 'I'm not sure that's a good idea. Your parents will be hostile if we make this too obvious. Besides, I said ages ago that I didn't want to take advantage of you while you're emotionally vulnerable and that still holds. I don't want to rush things. You're still in mourning.'

'You know what, I feel the same way. Mum and Dad are pretty old fashioned and already disapproving, and I still feel raw about the last couple of months so I'd rather we stayed just friends, for a while anyway ... so long as you still kiss me like you just did, from time to time ... '

'Like this, you mean?'

A couple of minutes later Charlie regained her balance. 'Where did you learn to kiss like that?' she laughed softly.

Matt looked away. 'I haven't exactly been celibate the last five years, you know. Nothing serious, though. You see, the trouble is, nobody matched up to you and so things soon ground to a halt with all of them. My heart wasn't in it and I didn't like to lead them on to nowhere.'

Charlie paused and felt his need to change the subject. 'By the way,' she said. 'I had a bit of a weird weekend trying to find Trev like you suggested.' She recounted what had happened, adding, 'Fine detective I'm turning out to be. But then, as a private person I don't have the same clout.'

'Maybe Trev has a criminal past and has decided to vanish for one reason or another, especially as he lied about owning that house. Can't you look him up on the Police National Computer or something?'

'Not on your nellie, unless I wanted to go to jail. It's a serious offence to misuse the PNC like that. I thought you knew that, since you're support staff.'

'Oh, yes, come to think of it, I was told that, but since I don't have access to that sort of thing I forgot.'

'I hope Trev turns up at the inquest. You all set for that? Because without Trev, you're the only witness to what he said over the phone. And there's the email, naturally.'

★　★　★

'Predictable I suppose,' Charlie said as she and Matt, and her mother and father left the inquest. Kent's family hadn't attended, which was just as well. It would have been galling to spend all that money on an air fare just to have the inquest adjourned. 'I'll have to phone Kent's parents and update them . . . hang it all, I might just email them. They haven't been exactly supportive in all of this. It also means I can think carefully about exactly what I want to say.'

'I want a cup of tea,' Charlie's mum said. 'I'm parched. Proper tea from a tea shop, mind, none of this fancy frothy coffee and dishwater with lemon muck.'

Charlie laughed. 'I think the Singing Kettle does a good old fashioned tea.' Matt looked as if he was about to take his leave but Charlie wanted him there for moral support. 'Lead on, please, Matt.'

'So what was all that about?' her dad asked when they were all seated in the teashop.

Charlie poured the tea as she

explained. 'The Coroner wanted Trev's testimony, unsurprisingly. He's the only witness to Kent's death. I had hoped Matt's testimony about the phone call and the email would be enough to declare Kent dead, but I can't say I'm really surprised that the Coroner adjourned it until Trev can bear witness.'

'That won't happen until Trev is found. Suppose he never turns up?' said Matt. 'Suppose he's decided never to come back? Suppose he was so freaked out he's topped himself?'

'Oh, do be quiet,' Charlie's dad barked. 'Your speculation isn't helping.'

Matt sulked into his teacup. 'Good job you said you thought Trev had moved, wasn't just ignoring the witness summons and in contempt of court. I hoped the coroner would relent then.'

'Not likely,' said Charlie. It was the outcome she had expected. 'It could be worse. The insurance company could have refused to cough up anything at all, then I really would have been up the creek. As it is, I'll get by, same as I did before. It does make it more urgent to find Trev though. I'll have a word with the Coroner's officer, see if she can help. It's a pity Trev didn't live nearer. It's a fair drive and we've suddenly got busy with a complex case at work, or I'd do some snooping myself.'

'Take an advert out in the nationals?' her mum suggested.

'Good idea but I bet it costs a packet.'

'Try Facebook,' said Matt. 'Or phone every lettings agent in the district. Surely now he's needed as a witness you can get people on to him. There must be something we can do.'

'The trouble is, although finding him as a witness is of paramount importance to us, in the great scheme of things it's just another in a long list of jobs for them,' said Charlie ruefully. 'The country's coroners are rather busy.'

Charlie's parents went home, and Charlie and Matt went back to the Big

House. They were very busy, both of them working on a massive fraud project that looked as if it might take several months to unravel.

At clocking-off time Matt came over to Charlie's department. 'I've been thinking,' he said. 'Why don't you come over on Saturday or Sunday and we can have a good look through Kent's things . . . if you can bear to, that is, maybe see if he's got any contacts for Trev? I haven't done anything with his personal stuff yet except hoard it. And why don't you ask Kent's parents if they have any ideas where Trev might be?'

Charlie pushed herself away from the computer and rubbed her eyes. 'Good idea. I'm not sure how I'll cope looking through Kent's things, though. As for his parents, I'm not even sure they knew Trev, apart from meeting him at the wedding. If we could find out where Trev worked, it would be a help.'

'Want to come out for a meal?'

Charlie considered the question. It

was very tempting because every moment spent in Matt's company was a pleasure. But her parents expected her home and she was tired, very tired, and needed some time to chill out and think without romantic distractions.

'Thanks, but I haven't finished what I'm doing here yet, and I'm too tired. And I need to send Kent's parents that email.'

*　　*　　*

Charlie stared at the computer screen, frowning at Kent's father's reply. It was abrupt to the point of rudeness, scathing about the way Britain worked, glad he now lived in the US and that for a detective she showed a complete lack of know-how when it came to the simple job of finding Trev.

It was as if his family were blaming her for their loss. Illogical, but not an uncommon reaction. *They're grieving*, she told herself. *They don't know the darker side of their precious son, apart*

140

from the debt which they wouldn't help out over. I loved him, but for me it's a relatively new thing. They've loved him since the day he was born, unconditionally. They're just lashing out because it makes them feel less guilty, she told herself.

They ought to remember that I'm grieving too, she thought, *but then they think I'm a roughty-toughty hardboiled copper.*

As for the gibe about not finding Trev, that was so unfair. She didn't even know he was missing until she went to see him.

She put her head in her arms on her desk and wept. She felt better for it, went downstairs and watched mindless TV with her parents before going to bed early.

7

Matt gave Charlie a hug as she arrived early on Saturday. 'First things first,' he said. 'Coffee. I've laid out all Kent's belongings in one of the bedrooms, and I've set up his computer and had a fair old snoop through that but without much success I'm afraid. Trev wasn't on Facebook.'

He switched the kettle on. The coffee things were already laid out. As they waited for the kettle to boil he gave her another hug, but seemed to sense she didn't want a passionate kiss, not before this unhappy task ahead.

He poured the water into the cafetière. 'I have opened up every email to and from Trev, looking to see if they were CC'd to anyone else, anyone who might know more about Trev, but no luck.' He gave the coffee a stir with a wooden spoon and the grounds started to settle.

'I've been racking my brains to think what Trev does for a living. He said he was in retail, I think . . . you know what it's like when you listen politely to someone but you're not actually that interested in what they have to say?' said Charlie. 'I can't remember if he said he works in a shop, owns a shop, or if he's a salesman or something. I wish now I'd paid more attention. One thing I did find out is that Trev definitely came home from Thailand. He was on one of the flights back from Bangkok.'

'How did you manage that?'

'I had a long chat with the Coroner's officer yesterday.'

'The who-what?' Matt pushed the plunger down then poured the coffee. 'Biscuit?'

'Ta.' Charlie helped herself to a biscuit. 'The Coroner's officer. She's a support staff officer employed by our police force but linked to the Coroner's office. A sort of go-between. There was a list of passengers for each flight, and

Trev was on the list, passed through customs. But where he went after that, goodness knows. It looks as if he stopped renting his house and vanished. Or if he owns it, he let it and vanished. Maybe he went a bit odd. I'm beginning to get concerned about him now. The Coroner's officer said it would be helpful if we could find him because they're rather stretched. These things take time.'

'That's useful. Mind you, I don't see why we should do their job for them.'

'Because we want closure . . . just like everyone else in this situation. To us, finding Trev and getting Kent declared dead is important. To them it's just another inquest.'

Once settled in Matt's arms drinking her coffee, Charlie found herself glued to the sofa. The minutes slid past and the coffee was finished and still they didn't make a move. It was just too nice snuggled together.

Eventually Matt stirred. 'Better get on with it, I suppose. Are you sure you're up to it? I mean, it's bound to be a bit raw.'

Charlie shook her head. 'I think so. I think it's part of letting go. I just wish I could mourn him without feeling angry.'

There were several cardboard boxes of clutter. Magazines and post were crammed randomly into boxes. 'For a man who said he was a minimalist, this is a lot of tat,' said Matt.

'His idea of tidying up was to shove it all in a box or a cupboard out of sight. Out of sight, out of mind. Then of course, it would be impossible come the next cardboard box-filling tidy-up session and he'd throw stuff out without even looking through it. And that's not the half of it,' Charlie told him. 'Some of these boxes were in storage from when his parents went to the States and we never even opened them, just shoved them in the spare bedroom when we got them out of storage. He was supposed to look through them and throw the rubbish away, but he never did.'

'In hindsight, it's a good job we didn't charity-shop it as your parents wanted,' Matt said.

'That row was awful, wasn't it? It was only the clothing that I think they thought I should dump. They knew I wanted to sift through the clutter in case there are mementoes I want to keep. I need to do this task anyway, even if we didn't want to find Trev.'

She stacked up the magazines and mail into separate piles. Some of the magazines hadn't even been opened.

'No wonder he racked up such debts,' said Matt. 'Sorry, I didn't mean to criticise, but he has loads of magazines here, and they're not exactly cheap, some of them.'

'Quite,' Charlie agreed, opening an envelope. 'Talking of debt, I've found an old credit card bill in one of these boxes in storage. He owed big time back in 2002. He always gave the impression of being well-off, but looks as if it was all borrowed.'

Matt opened his mouth to say something, then closed it, looked away. 'It's awful. I just want to moan about him but we shouldn't speak ill of the dead.'

'Why not?' said Charlie. 'There's a certain basic dishonesty in pretending he was Mr Perfect. I thought he was, and he wasn't. I still loved him, though, and I still miss him dreadfully, even though . . . '

She started crying, silently, then brushed the tears away angrily. 'What's done is done. The debts are paid and don't mean anything any more. If I get the rest of the life insurance that's a bonus, but I don't need it. I don't really need that death certificate. Not in a practical way.'

'Not at the moment, maybe, but you can't get married again until you're officially a widow.'

Charlie rocked back on her heels. 'I hadn't thought of that; I'm being pretty stupid at the moment. Of course I can't.' She stood up stiffly. 'My knees are killing me. We should take one box downstairs at a time, and do this sitting at the dining table.'

'Okay.'

Matt picked up a box to carry downstairs while Charlie put the kettle on. It wasn't until she was waiting for it to boil that she wondered if her being a widow mattered to Matt . . . was he thinking of marriage?

Matt sorted out the magazines into date order and tied them with string. 'I could try flogging them; a car boot sale perhaps, and it always looks better if you have a year's worth.'

'It's not worth the hassle. We can charity-shop this lot once it's sorted. It was the designer stuff I was concerned about, especially when I was so scared of that debt.'

They continued sifting though the boxes until most of it was sorted. There was a random assortment of credit card bills and bank statements, mostly hidden in magazines, some unopened.

'I'm angry now,' Charlie said firmly.

'Suppose I had just gathered these magazines up and sent them to the charity shop or recycling without looking? Anyone could have got the joint credit card account details — and I bet Kent wouldn't have even noticed any discrepancies because I bet he had his head well in the sand with all this.'

'Maybe, but I expect he meant to sort it out and wouldn't have chucked magazines out without looking. I shouldn't think he expected to die . . . '

'He was a soldier, Matt. It kind of goes with the territory,' she corrected him solemnly. 'But I don't suppose he ever thought it would really happen, and I bet he never gave those he would be leaving behind a moment's thought either. Whatever did I see in him?'

'He was a nice bloke, Charlie,' Matt answered sadly. 'And fun to be with. I liked him when we were at school. He was my best friend. Let's not lose sight of that.'

He stood, walked round the table to her and hugged her from behind, kissed the top of her head. 'Let's have a look at one more box, then have something to eat. It's way past lunchtime. I'll go fetch another box.'

While he was upstairs Charlie idly flicked through a scuba diving magazine. 'These are the most amazing photos,' she said to Matt as he came downstairs with a box that looked very battered and saggy. 'I can understand why Kent and Trev liked it so much.' Suddenly, she froze. 'Diving! They must have been members of the same club. I wonder . . .'

'Food first,' said Matt. 'I'm famished and I bet you are. I'll make some tuna sarnies if you like.' He looked down at his hands. 'Ugh. Why is it that boxes stored in lofts get so filthy?'

Charlie wasn't feeling hungry until she bit into the first sandwich, then she realised that she was ravenous.

'I'm going to look online for diving clubs while you look through that last box,' Matt suggested.

Charlie slit the brown tape holding

the box closed. It was one of the ones that Kent had had in storage since his family went to the States, and from the looks of it had been up in their loft for a long time before that.

It was a strong carton but even so was looking flaccid, tatty and very dusty. Inside was some old A-Level notes, a couple of photo albums, a sports trophy, and some certificates, like Best Cadet, which he'd won on one summer camp. There were a few aeroplane models, and some magazines and comics, and his old beret from when they were cadets.

Charlie found herself flicking through the albums. She found a photograph of her twelve-year-old self, with Matt and Kent and the rest of the cadets. They'd joined the first year of secondary school. The cadet corps was attached to the school, a long-term hangover from when it had been a boys' grammar school. As she flicked through, each photograph evoked memories.

Matt had come to stand behind her.

'I remember that summer camp. That's when Mad Max Higgins came back to camp after going to the pub and getting blitzed and got thrown in the jug house until his folks came to collect him.'

'I'd forgotten that,' she said.

'I remember the smell of Kent's feet after a long hot walk once. We thought he'd hidden his cheese rations in his boots.'

'I remember when Kent tied the top of your sleeping bag closed and you couldn't get out. He'd used my bootlaces, the idiot, and I had a job undoing them.'

Charlie turned a few more pages, pages full of memories and people long moved on. 'I wonder where they all are now,' she mused. She looked up at Matt.

Tears were glistening in his eyes. 'They were good times, Charlie. We had such hopes, such ideals. We thought we were heroes, but only Kent was.'

'He was and he wasn't, Matt. We all felt like heroes, but when it came to it you and I picked different jobs and when Kent was tested he found he wasn't as brave as he thought he should be . . . Let me tell you what he told me about Simbo.'

'Are you sure . . . ?'

'You were his best mate and I think you should know. When Kent came back from Iraq he wasn't the same. Just before Christmas I found out why . . . '

When Charlie had finished telling Matt her story he seemed to be made of wood, he was so still. He was hardly breathing, looking into the distance.

'He was brave, in spite of that, Charlie,' he said finally. 'He was brave just to even go. I don't think I could do that, don't think when it came to the crunch I could ever be brave enough. Despite all he did with the emails and stuff, despite how he felt about Simbo, he was still a hero.'

'I want to keep these things. I'll find a proper box for them, but do you mind if I leave them here?' asked Charlie.

'Of course. I have a strongbox they

could go in. I wouldn't mind looking through some of those photos myself if that's okay.' He disappeared upstairs, returning with a metal box.

Charlie carefully laid the photo albums and certificates into the box. 'Nobody will want these old comics or magazines, will they? I'm going to hang onto the trophies and stuff, though; they remind me of the good times together.'

Matt peeped into the tatty cardboard box. 'Is that it?'

'There are some old mobile phones. Real bricks. I'm not sure if they can be recycled any more.'

'Wow! Shows you how far mobiles have come since they first came out. I remember my dad had an early one and it really was like a brick. And the Thing To Be was a mobile phone salesman.'

He pulled them out of the box and matched the chargers to the phones. 'There's nothing wrong with them, they're perfectly good phones. I think some charities refurbish them for Third

World countries.'

He went into the kitchen and came back with some strong polythene bags, put each phone plus its charger in a bag. Then he picked up one of the two without chargers, and frowned.

'I remember . . . ' He turned it on, but the battery was flat, unsurprisingly. He flicked the back off one of the phones, removed the SIM card, and put it in his own phone.

'Proof, if ever proof were needed . . . look.'

Charlie looked. 'What am I supposed to be looking at?'

'My stored numbers are on this SIM card, including yours. I thought I recognised the model. And this one,' Matt picked up the fourth phone. 'Is that the same type of phone as you lost that time, just before the scammy email Kent sent?'

Charlie picked it up. It looked familiar. She nodded silently and handed the phone back to Matt. He did the same trick with the SIM card.

'Yes, look, here's my old home phone number. So Kent did nick them. That email wasn't just an impulse, then, it was a well-planned operation to get us split up so he could muscle in on you. What a cunning fox.'

Charlie stood abruptly. 'I need some fresh air.'

They dressed up warmly because as soon as the sun went down it would get cold, and walked down the road towards the path into the woods.

'What a massive hedge,' said Matt as they walked past one house. A huge Leylandii hedge swamping the front garden.

'That's Sue's. She doesn't mind the hedge because it stops people looking into her front room as they walk past.'

Matt shuddered. 'I'd find it claustrophobic.'

The woods were showing signs of spring; bluebell leaves starting to spear their way through last year's leaf litter.

Charlie soon felt herself calming down with the rhythm of walking. As usual she and Matt were perfectly in step, just as they had been as cadets when hillwalking.

'How do you feel?' he asked. 'I mean, about all this; memories and finding out nasty truths like this?'

Charlie stopped. 'To be honest Matt, I don't know how I feel. Just as I think I'm getting to the point where I can cope something else comes along. I thought I knew him so well, but now it seems I never really knew him at all. I think I've reached the point where I can't take any more in. You know, I still get the feeling this is all unreal and that he'll walk through the front door larger than life with that sexy grin of his.'

Matt was gazing at her intently. She brushed his wayward lock of hair from his eyes. 'And then sometimes it seems like it was my three months of marriage that was all a dream.'

Matt lowered his lips to hers, brushed them lightly with his. 'You are the most beautiful, wonderful creature.' He kissed her. Charlie knew the chemistry between them was right, felt that things were going to get more intimate and she welcomed the thought — but Matt pulled away.

'What's wrong?' she asked.

'We're all stirred up emotionally, both if us. I want to, how I want to, but it still feels wrong somehow. When it feels right, then . . . ' He looked aside. 'I want Kent's ghost laid to rest before I . . . You know what I'm saying, don't you, Charlie darling?'

Charlie knew.

★ ★ ★

It was late when they got back to the house. 'I'd better go,' Charlie said. 'Mum's expecting me for supper and she'd be scandalised if I stayed the night, though staying would make sense because I'd like to carry on where we left off tomorrow.'

Matt laughed. 'Left off where?'

'Here,' she said and kissed him briefly. 'Though I actually meant with sorting stuff out and looking for Trev.'

'I've started a list of local scuba clubs and lettings agents. I've also one or two other ideas up my sleeve. Perhaps you should have asked Trev's neighbours if they know where he works and who the letting agent is.'

'Crumbs, what a fool! Of course I should. Told you I think my brain's gone AWOL.'

'If we have time tomorrow perhaps we could pop over there, try again. You could lean on the new tenants, tell them he's in contempt of court or something. Flash your warrant card at them. Impress them with your lovely legs.'

She laughed. 'Somehow I don't think my legs will impress that grumpy new mother.'

8

As Charlie drove back to her parents' house she found her thoughts and memories swirling like a blizzard until softly, one by one they settled down, leaving her in a state of calm acceptance. She thought perhaps it was because she'd had to focus utterly on the driving, pushing the thoughts to one side.

Her mum greeted her rather too jovially, offered a sherry before dinner, which was a relatively new habit on her part, but one which Charlie appreciated.

It was roast lamb, one of Charlie's favourite dishes, and she was glad she hadn't stayed over at Matt's. Besides, Matt was right. Everything was too recent and too raw, especially with each new surprise, and she wasn't sure what she wanted. She was sure she wanted

Matt, but not as a furtive affair burdened with guilt. She knew they would become lovers at some point. It was just a question of when.

Just as her thoughts were settling down, Aunty Sophie phoned. Charlie updated her on the parts of her life she wanted to share, then her aunt cleared her throat. 'And how's your financial situation?' she asked. 'You coping okay? If I can help out in any way . . . '

'Thanks,' said Charlie. 'But I'm getting by now I'm at Mum and Dad's and Matt's renting my place. It's cool.'

★ ★ ★

'You are gonna love me,' said Matt the next morning as he answered the door. He looked as excited as a puppy, which made Charlie laugh.

'I already do.'

'I am a techno hero.' Matt raised his hands and swivelled his hips. 'Let me show you what I found . . . Ta-da . . . One list of local scuba clubs. And this one is the one Trev and Kent were both members of. I phoned and explained, and they said that Kent hadn't been on a dive for ages — before his tour in Iraq presumably, but Trev had been on a couple last autumn, but nobody has seen or heard from him since Christmas. The person I spoke to got a bit cagey then and wouldn't say anything more because he realised I could be anyone . . . I said we'd pop over and see him later if that's okay with you.'

Matt flicked his hair back before Charlie could get to it.

'Well done, that's a great starting point.'

'Next, I put Trev's email address into a search engine and found a scuba forum. I tried a search on 'Trevor Hardwick' plus 'scuba diving' and got nothing, but that's because they use usernames. Trev is Hardboy5 — don't laugh! — he stopped posting and hasn't been back since before Christmas.

'And I got a list of letting agents ready. I think we should have a coffee, then go. We'll speak to Mr Scuba, then go and talk to Trev's neighbours, then if that draws a blank we'll talk to the letting agents. I hope you brought your warrant card.'

'A warrant card isn't a magic wand, you know, and neither should it be misused.'

'But you're not misusing it. If Trev is needed as a witness then I don't see why you shouldn't look for him, and it's mainly a good form of ID so that people know we are who we say we are. I'm not surprised they're being a bit cagey. You can't be too careful nowadays.'

* * *

The diving club chairman, Mr Jenkins met them at the clubhouse, which was rather more swish than Charlie had expected. She'd imagined a shack with neoprene diving suits and battered aqualungs, but it was a modern and burglar-proof looking building with a classy eatery attached.

Mr Jenkins ushered them to his office. 'Sorry I sounded so suspicious over the phone, but we had a problem a while back with someone asking after one of our members. Said he was a friend trying to track down this member for a school reunion, and it wasn't that at all. It was a journalist after a story because this member was accused of something very untoward.'

'I quite understand, Mr Jenkins. Let me tell you a little about myself, and why I'm so interested in Trev,' Charlie explained.

She gave him a brief résumé, then finished up with, 'Although Trev is needed as a witness in Kent's inquest and I am a police officer, I'm seeing you as a private individual, but here's my warrant card to prove who I am. You told Matt that Trev hasn't been here since before Christmas, is that right?'

'Yup. He might have joined another club, though. He was thinking of doing so. Kent was his dive buddy, so it might be that Trev has lost all stomach for the sport after that dreadful tsunami. I've taken his file out and had a look through to see if there's anything that might help. This is confidential and no way would I normally do this.'

He showed Charlie the sheet. It had Trev's address, date of birth, and interestingly, some next of kin listed. An aunt and uncle who lived in Fort William. Charlie noted their address and phone number down, as well as that of Trev's GP.

'You've been enormously helpful and I can't thank you enough,' she said.

'I hope he's okay,' Mr Jenkins said. 'I was sorry to hear he had such a rough time in Thailand, and I'm really sorry for your loss. If Trev pitches up I'll tell him you're looking for him, or tell him to get in touch with the Coroner's office.'

'Please do,' said Charlie, 'Here's my card and the Coroner's office has a website . . . ' She wrote the website address on the back of her card. 'I've had to use my police business card because that's all I have on me, but remember — this is not official police business.'

* * *

'Where first?' asked Matt as they reached the town nearest Trev's house.

'Coffee,' said Charlie immediately. 'I need a coffee.'

'You only just had one an hour and a bit ago.'

'Yes, I need to get rid of that one and fill up again.'

'Ah, okay.' Matt followed the signs to a car park, a different one from the one Charlie used, and they wandered towards the coffee shop she remembered. On the way they passed an estate agent's — again, a different one from before. Charlie glanced at the display of properties briefly.

'Stop a minute, Matt. That photo in the window looks like Trev's house . . . there, the one saying, *SOLD: More properties like this needed.'*

'Are you sure?'

'Yes, I think so.'

'Okay, let's go in and ask them about it.'

'After a coffee, or I won't be able to concentrate.'

'Caffeine addict,' Matt teased.

Matt fetched coffee while Charlie made herself comfortable. 'Did you get the right house when you came up last?' he said.

'Yes, I know I did.'

'So the house was sold . . . it looks as if it was Trev's as he said, and that woman was wrong. Maybe the person who bought it, let it. You know; buy-to-let, the new savings plan.'

'Looks like it.' Charlie poked at the cap on her cappuccino with her spoon, playing with the foam. Then she scooped some into her mouth. It tasted of nothing; her mind was far away.

'In which case,' Matt pondered, 'the list of letting agents is a waste of time because the letting agent won't know where Trev is, nor have a forwarding address for him because he wasn't the previous tenant, nor is he the landlord if it's been sold and then let.' he frowned. 'Did that make any sense?'

'You're burbling but I understood.' The coffee was getting cold so she drank it. 'Hopefully they can give us a bit of info.'

Matt's hand slid across the table until it brushed hers. He squeezed it. 'Don't be too despondent. He'll turn up eventually.'

Charlie's mobile rang; she answered, listened in silence then said, 'That's weird, very interesting. Thanks for this. We'll exchange notes when I see you.'

She hung up then said to Matt, 'That was my chum, the Coroner's officer. She says she found out who Trev was working for — and get this; Trev chucked in his job without even going back to it after he got back from Phuket. Just sent an email to his boss who, apparently, wasn't best pleased. That's just weird. I think he's had an emotional meltdown. Poor Trev.'

Matt drained his cup. 'Like you say; weird. Let's talk to the estate agent, then, and if they're not helpful I think you should lean on them. I'll be the muscle.' He backed this up with a wink.

'Idiot,' Charlie laughed.

The estate agent's had a gentleman about Charlie's father's age sitting behind a computer terminal. He stood immediately with a smile and said. 'Good morning, how can I help?' which Charlie took as a good sign.

'I hope you can help. The situation is this . . . ' Charlie gave the same sort of explanation she'd given Mr Jenkins, and it seemed to work its magic this time, too. Of course, talking to men rather than women sometimes roused the gallant in them.

'I see your problem,' said the estate agent. 'Obviously much of this is confidential information and I'm not at liberty to breach that confidence, but I can say that the vendor was indeed called Trevor Hardwick. It was an unusually rapid sale because the price was very competitive and there was no onward chain. The purchaser was, as you surmised, wanting a property to let; a cash buyer. It was an excellent property, no problems with the survey and the time between exchange of contracts and completion was barely three weeks.

'There was, as far as I can see, nothing dodgy about the deal, as the monies were deposited into Mr Hardwick's bank account. Mr Hardwick senior was well known to me before his tragic accident, but I hadn't seen Trev since he was a little boy, must be . . . ' the estate agent tilted his head. 'Bless me, it must be twenty years, possibly more. I remember him sitting in this very office fidgeting on his mother's knee as his father purchased that house. A lovely property.'

'Did Trev say why he was selling up?' Matt asked.

'Bad memories? Perhaps he wanted to start a new life, maybe buy a different house with the lever of being a cash buyer, maybe see the world a bit. I must say he did look a bit drained.'

'Was there a forwarding address?'

'The George and Dragon — it's a pub and hotel on the outskirts of town. I don't suppose he's there now. This was a few weeks back.'

'Thank you so much, you've been very helpful. If you remember anything else, could you ring me, please?' She gave the man her card, adding her personal mobile number. 'Call my personal number, not my work number, unless it's urgent.'

'I have a map of the town and I'll mark the George and Dragon on it. But I expect he's gone by now. Sorry.'

'Who was his conveyancing solicitor?' asked Matt.

'I'm sorry, but I'm not disclosing that information — not unless you can give me a very good reason for doing so.'

★ ★ ★

The landlord remembered Trev, showed them his signature in the visitor's book, and no, he didn't leave a forwarding address.

Back at the car, after another cup of coffee, Charlie let out a big sigh. 'You know what I think? I think Trev faced his own mortality in Phuket and he's cashed in so he can have a rollicking good time in case he dies suddenly. He's gone off the rails a bit — understandable. I might feel exactly the same under the circumstances, especially if he has no ties.'

'He has got ties; his aunt and uncle.'

'I meant no dependents.'

Matt did his seatbelt up. 'Where now, McDuff? Do we talk to the neighbours?'

Charlie thought for a minute or two, checked her watch. 'Yes, why not? We've come all this way.'

'Blimey,' said Matt as they drew up at Trev's old house. 'That's a bit posher than I was expecting. Trev must be rolling in it. It's a lovely house. I wouldn't have sold it.'

'I wish I knew Trev a bit better. It does seem an odd thing to do but maybe it reminds him too much of his parents. I don't think I'd have liked to have carried on living in the house on the base; it would have brought back too many memories — happy memories, it's true, but happy memories made the sadness seem sadder.'

Matt's hand found hers.

'Maybe . . . ' continued Charlie, 'Maybe he found after all the horrors of Phuket he couldn't bear living in the house his parents were in. Or here's a thought — maybe he wanted to give the money to the emergency fund.'

'That's a thought. But surely he'd tell someone; friends . . . '

'Maybe he has, but we don't know who his friends are.'

'I think we should talk to his old mates in the regiment.'

'So many things to do, so many people to speak to. And not that much time. We'll just have to chip away slowly at this problem, and hope that Trev gets the message that his testimony is needed.'

There was a man of about sixty cutting the lawn in the front garden of the house next door to Trev's. He'd paused, engine idling, and was looking at them a little quizzically. Charlie smiled at him and went through her usual spiel.

The man looked sympathetic. 'I saw lights on in the house after Christmas so I presume he came home all right, but I didn't see him except at a distance. I saw the car going in and out a few times, the For Sale sign and one of those removals vans, only it said House Clearance on the side.

'I was a bit put out, to be honest, because he didn't say a word to us, but not everyone likes to tell people they're selling up in case everyone else follows suit. I had that happen to me once. Put our house on the market, everyone saw what the asking price was and started getting the same idea.

'Let me ask the wife if she knows anything.'

They followed the man round to the back door where he yelled for his wife to come out. 'She'll kill me if I tread grass clippings into the house.'

His wife came to the back door.

'You explain,' said the man. 'It's a bit complicated.'

'Oh, you poor thing,' said his wife when Charlie finished. 'I didn't see him either. You don't during the winter because everyone stays indoors and it's so dark. Then he upped and moved sticks without so much as a goodbye. Maybe his head was turned with your husband dying like that. It was awful watching the news; God knows what it must have been like out there. Would you like a coffee?'

'How kind, but no thanks. Do you happen to remember any names on the removal van?'

The couple thought for a minute, then shook their heads. 'Not one I've seen in these parts,' said the man. 'Sorry.'

'Well, thanks anyway, sorry to have troubled you.'

'No trouble at all,' the wife said. 'I hope you find him. It must be dreadful for you, dear.'

The neighbours on the other side had a similar story to tell. They hadn't actually seen the removal/clearance van and had felt similarly miffed when Trev moved without saying goodbye.

'Known him since he was a wee nipper, him and his little sister,' said the lady of the house. 'Rude if you ask me, but then he got rude and surly when he became a teenager and joining the army like that. His mum wasn't happy, I can tell you.'

'Definitely gone off the rails, if you ask me,' said Charlie when they got back in the car. 'I'm not surprised. I thought his email was a bit abrupt and I'm annoyed he didn't have the courtesy to come and see me.

'It's like he's running away from his past. Oh well, I have enough to worry about without worrying about his mental health. Let's go home and phone up the aunt and uncle. I didn't know about the little sister. Why isn't she his next of kin?'

'Stop a mo . . . go back,' said Matt. He jumped out of the car, ran up to the second house, spoke to the couple again, then came back with a sad face.

'The little sister was killed in the same accident that killed Trev's parents. No wonder he sold the house. The tsunami must have been the last straw.'

'Poor bloke. I hope he hasn't done anything daft.'

★ ★ ★

When they got back home, Charlie phoned Trev's aunt and uncle's number. A youngish female voice answered. 'Mum and dad are out,' she said when Charlie asked for them. 'Can I help? You're not telesales, are you?'

Charlie laughed. 'You sound like you hate them as much as I do. I'm actually looking for Trevor Hardwick and I wonder if you've heard from him lately.'

'My cousin? No. Not for a couple of

years. Saw him the Christmas before last. Why?'

Charlie explained, starting with Trev being the best man at her wedding, and ending with the adjourned inquest.

'I never knew he was out there then,' breathed the girl. 'Oh, poor Trev — and poor you. I'm sorry for your loss,' she added in a slightly stilted formal way. 'Crumbs.'

'Have you an address, mobile number, anything?'

The girl gave Charlie Trev's old address and phone number — no mobile number. 'I'll ask Mum and Dad if they know anything when they get home.'

★ ★ ★

Charlie's mum was very clucky when she got back to her parents' house, wanting to know where she'd been, how she'd done, so Charlie gave an account over the evening meal.

She didn't bother telling them about

the discovery of the mobile phones, but did mention the photographs. She'd brought one back, a framed photo of herself standing between Matt and Kent. It brought back poignant memories and seemed symbolic of the way she felt.

After helping to clear up, she said, 'I'm going to have a long soak and an early night, if you don't mind. I'm shattered and I think I'm suffering from information overload.'

Sleep eluded her at first.

Without Trev's testimony unless Kent was disinterred and identified, he could not be declared dead. She'd done her best to find him, but now she was beginning to wonder if it was worth it. Perhaps it was time to stop looking and concentrate on more important things, like work — like Matt.

She didn't need an official declaration of death — not really.

Not yet, anyway.

9

'You've got tomato sauce on your shirt,' said Charlie accusingly in the Italian restaurant.

Matt looked down in mock dismay. 'Oh no, clean on as well. Mind you, my shirts are clean on every day. Mum would never serve spag bol if the table cloth was a fresh one because you could bet that I'd muck it up.'

'How are your parents? Settled in yet?'

'Good, thanks. Dad loves his new job and Mum seems to have made some new friends. What about yours?'

'Still smothering me with love and affection. I think they're getting a bit suspicious of so much late-night working. I'm terrified they'll phone me at work and I won't be there. I've told them to use my mobile because the phones need to be kept free for emergencies.'

'Crafty . . .'

'And not strictly true, but I don't want them phoning up our direct line and then getting in a flap because I don't answer.'

'Mmm,' Matt murmured in agreement, wiping bread over his plate. He put his hand on the table and she reached out for it. His eyes glittered in the candlelight.

'I'm not sure I like all the subterfuge, but I don't want Mum and Dad getting hot under the collar about things. They thought Kent was wonderful, you know,' she said.

'As opposed to me.'

'I'm not sure they were convinced about the email thing.'

'We could show them, if you like.'

Charlie shook her head, pulling in a breath over her teeth. 'No. I only said it was a mistake. I haven't told them Kent did it deliberately. What's the point in letting them know? It would only upset them; besmirching Kent's memory. I know, you know, and that's

181

what's important.'

Charlie couldn't have told anyone what the rest of the conversation was that night; all she could remember was a warm glow and Matt's smiling face.

She felt contented, and she knew in her heart it felt right.

As they stood up to leave they saw a couple of people from the Big House looking at them.

'Uh-oh, I bet they gossip,' said Matt.

'I bet. Bother. Perhaps we shouldn't have meals out in town, perhaps we should just cook at the house. I ought to come over and help sort the garden out, anyway. I like gardening.'

'I like the power tools. Grrrraaaaaarrr,' said Matt, pretending to wield a hedge-trimmer.

★　★　★

A couple of days later, Charlie's mother almost jumped on her when she came home. 'You're going out with that Matt, aren't you?' she accused. 'You're the gossip of the village, I can tell you. You were seen in Pandleford at the cinema, all over him like a rash, by all accounts.'

'Good grief, not only are the gossipmongers out in force, they're prone to exaggeration as well. He's a work colleague, and an old friend, and he's been very supportive of late. We're working late on the same project — you know he does computer forensics — he looks at suspects' computers for us. We went to the cinema to chill out.'

'So you *are* going out with him. Kent's only been dead four months and you're making out with an old flame. Don't you think that's a bit disrespect-ful?'

'Mum, if I were 'making out' with him I'd be living in my house with him openly, not living here. If anyone's being disrespectful it's the old biddies sitting in judgement on us when actually they don't know the half of it. I'm going out with him as a friend, not a lover. I get tired of this sort of trial by gossip and I really wish you wouldn't listen to such boll — balderdash. Now I'm tired, I've had rather an intense day and I need to relax.'

'You're a fool if you think you love him. You're five years older than when you were going out with him as kids — older and should be wiser. He's caught you on the rebound and he's only after you for your house and what he can get . . . I remember what a vulture he was over Kent's clothes.'

Her mum spoke fiercely and clamped her lips in a hard line.

'Mum! Listen to me. Kent bought expensive designer clothes he couldn't afford on credit cards and left my position so precarious by a despicable act of fraud, that I would have had to sell my house if he hadn't had life insurance.

'Matt was right — he managed to sell some of those clothes and he gave me the money which helped stave off destitution.' Finally, Charlie had had too much and she blurted out, 'He's a good man, is Matt, sensitive and considerate — and I wish I'd married him and not Kent, because at the end of the day Kent was utterly selfish, and I suspect he would have made me very unhappy in the long run!'

'You're glad he's dead, glad . . . ' Her mother's mouth was an aghast, exaggerated O-shape.

'No — that's not what I meant! But there were secrets, Mum, secrets and lies that I only found out about after . . . ' Her frustration was building. 'Look, I've had enough of this. There's no point in rowing. I'm going out with Matt as a friend and maybe, eventually, as something more, and that's that.'

Charlie brushed past her mother and stomped upstairs. There was no lock on her door so she did as she had as a child, sat with her back to the door, muttering and going over the row in forensic detail.

She wanted to phone Aunty Sophie — but she wasn't sure whose side she'd be on.

* * *

Charlie knocked on DI Benton's door and poked her head around the door, looking into the room.

'Ma'am, can I have a chat? In confidence, please?

'Yes of course. Come in and shut the door.' DI Benton rested her chin on the thumbs of her clasped hands. 'How can I help?'

'It's difficult, not really a police matter, but I need someone's opinion, someone not too close to the situation like my Mum and Aunty. It's like this . . . '

Charlie explained everything, including Kent's perfidious emails and his fraudulent credit card behaviour.

'You see,' she added, 'I'm worried that Mum, Dad and Aunty Sophie are right and that I'm vulnerable at the moment, that I'm falling in love with Matt just because of what happened between us five years ago. I suppose I'm worried I might be making another mistake.'

'Another? Was marrying Kent a mistake, then?'

'No, I loved him. And I suppose if Matt hadn't appeared, I wouldn't be any the wiser and I might have been happier.'

'I see,' said DI Benton in a way that implied she saw a great deal indeed. 'So what's the problem, then . . . if you'll forgive me, Kent is missing, very much presumed dead, so what's to stop you and Matt being lovers?'

'Mum and Dad . . . I know I'm an adult, but at the same time I don't want to hurt their feelings. They keep on going on about being caught on the rebound and trying to relive old childhood love, and it's got me doubting myself. The biggest part of me is in love with Matt, but their words are causing niggling doubts and it's like a slow poison.

'And the other thing is, I want to marry Matt, but we can't because we don't have a death certificate for Kent.'

'You can ask for an inquest without a

body, you know. I'm sure that would be granted under the circumstances.'

'We asked, one was granted, but when the Coroner heard that Trev was the one who told us Kent was dead, he adjourned it until Trev can give evidence — and Trev has vanished. Sold his house up, and vanished. He doesn't even know that his evidence is needed.'

'Really?' said DI Benton quietly, looking into the middle distance. 'How interesting. How did you find out that Trev's house has been sold?'

Charlie explained what she and Matt had found out.

'There are other things I could do, I suppose, and if he were a suspect I could use different avenues, but I've just had enough of it for the moment. I think I'll just let things happen in their own good time. Trev'll turn up sooner or later, and if he doesn't, then too bad. I feel a bit sorry for his aunt and uncle and cousins though, because they now know that he's disappeared. Do you think Trev's had a breakdown?'

'I suppose that could be it. I suppose it's enough to turn anyone's head . . . Forgive me, I haven't quite understood what relationship Trev and Kent had with each other . . . why did he go on the holiday, not you?'

'I couldn't, ma'am, if you recall, because I was due in court.'

'Oh, that's right.'

Charlie didn't think her boss had forgotten. Somehow this conversation wasn't going at all the way she expected. Charlie had hoped for someone to smooth her ruffled feathers, perhaps give her permission to fall in love, reassure her it was okay.

Instead, she found a strong feeling of disquiet growing, one that she couldn't explain because she didn't know why she was feeling uneasy.

'We're snookered until Trev turns up,' she told DI Benton. 'Though I suppose we could argue that, since there's been enough time for Kent to surface and he hasn't, he could be presumed dead.'

'You and Matt could always just live together,' DI Benton suggested absent-mindedly.

'True, but in the long term we would want to get married because of pension rights and so on, quite apart from, what if we want to have kids? And anyhow, we want to make a proper commitment to each other.'

'Was this Trev the one who was best man at the wedding?'

'Yes, that's right.'

'I remember chatting to him . . . nice young man. Can I look at your wedding photographs? Bring them in tomorrow. Perhaps we could ask people to keep an eye open for him, on the quiet. There are things we can do and once Trev gives his evidence then you can get Kent's death certificate and find proper closure and be free to marry Matt.'

'Yes, ma'am, I'll do that. And I appreciate talking to you. It's helped me straighten out my own thoughts.'

'Good, because things are going to get very busy with this present case, and I want you to be able to get on with the job in hand without getting distracted. Leave it with me, Charlie.'

10

'I've had enough,' Charlie said to Matt as they walked hand in hand through the bluebell woods. 'Mum is driving me absolutely nuts. I want to move into the house, even if we don't actually sleep together.'

'And how hard will that be, love?' Matt clasped her to his chest and she felt his heart pounding next to hers as he kissed her. 'I love you, I want you — I'm not sure I could keep my hands off you if we slept in the same house.'

'Well, then, let's just live together. Kent's dead, Matt; we don't need a certificate to know that. I love you, I've always loved you. Even when I loved Kent, I still had a corner in my heart for you. And when I met you on the train that day, I wished . . .

'But it was too late, everything was organised, and at the time I thought you'd dumped me, so I carried on, telling myself it was the right thing, when all the time, my heart was telling me something different.

'I know we'd both rather get married, and I can't bear the thought of never being able to marry you just because that ragbag Trev hasn't had the decency to call by and tell me what happened — who thinks it's okay to tell me news like that in a one-minute phone call to you and an email.

'He could have come to see me when he got back, Matt, and explain. But instead he expected me to tell Kent's family, his friends, and now he's vanished, leaving us in this mess . . . '

Charlie buried her face in Matt's chest and sobbed. He held her, feeling her muscles tense with all the strain of the events of the last few weeks.

Finally, she lifted her head to look up at him. 'So I've decided, Matt — I'm not waiting any longer.'

'I know, love, I know . . . shhh . . . I love you, you know that. Move in with me, then. It's your house after all, and damn the world and its opinions. I'll buy you a ring to show my commitment to you, and then when we're able, we'll get married properly.'

His voice was husky with emotion and Charlie saw the gleam of tears on his lashes. As he kissed her, the bluebells swirled into a mass of indigo, their scent as intoxicating as his kiss.

★ ★ ★

The sea swirled gently over the sand and over Charlie's and Matt's toes. Charlie squealed and said, 'It's freezing! I'm not swimming in that!'

Matt was laughing. 'Me neither.'

They backed up the beach then walked along, hand in hand.

Charlie kept casting looks at Matt. He'd stripped down to swimming trunks, showing how surprisingly muscular he was. There was no visible sign of it when he was clothed because he was slender, unlike Kent whose body had been slabs of in-your-face muscle. Matt was as graceful as a dancer, his muscles sharply sculpted under glowing skin.

She admired the way those muscles moved under his skin and a wave of desire washed through her, leaving her dizzy.

Though the sun was shining, it wasn't as warm as it first appeared and they put their clothes back on now they'd decided not to swim.

The sea was blue as sapphires and the sun deceptively warm on their faces. A light wind ruffled Matt's hair and Charlie smoothed it down.

He caught her to him, kissed her lips, then her forehead. 'You are so beautiful and I love you.'

'I love you, too,' she said softly, then broke away and laughed. 'Race you to the ice cream van. Loser pays.'

They pounded through the sand, neck and neck until Charlie just pipped Matt to the van.

'Okay, what do you want?' he asked.

'A double 99!'

'Greedy so-and-so!'

'Am not!' she laughed in reply, feeling carefree for the first time in way too long.

They walked back along the beach licking their ice creams.

'You've dropped a bit down your front — as usual, mucky pup,' said Charlie.

As Matt looked down she pushed his elbow a fraction and his nose buried itself in the ice cream. He pulled a face at her and she shrieked with laughter.

'I've a good mind to make you lick that off, you cheeky monkey,' he said, laughing.

Then suddenly, he stopped laughing, but the smile still played on his lips. 'That's the first time I've heard you laugh — really laugh like that — for ages . . . not since . . . well, not since we were kids . . . Happy?'

'Happy,' she beamed back.

'I know this sounds daft, but I want to build a sandcastle.' Matt's eyes were dancing with joy.

'Oh, yes, let's! We can buy a bucket and spade. I used to love doing that.'

They went to the parade of shops and bought a couple of buckets and spades and soon they were hard at it, building a huge sandcastle and decorating it with shells and pebbles.

Charlie had her back to the sea when suddenly she squealed and leapt up. The tide had turned, sneaking up on her.

'Mind the sandcastle,' Matt laughed. 'Let's watch the water fill up the moat.'

'I'm cold,' Charlie sulked with a little pout of her lips.

'We'll soon sort that,' said Matt, hugging her and holding her close to him.

The sea slid round their ankles and undermined the castle ramparts. The next wave made them retreat up the beach a pace or two, then farther as the next wave teased their toes again. The next wave buried the castle and all that was left when the wave retreated was a mound. As they backed up the beach they watched the sandcastle disappear beneath the waves.

'It's a bit symbolic,' observed Charlie, suddenly sober. 'My marriage was just a sandcastle and the sea took it all away in one day.' She shivered.

Matt took off his jacket and wrapped it round her shoulders. 'I'm so sorry,' he told her. 'I should have thought. What a fool I was to bring you here . . . it's just that I used to love this place when I was a kid.'

'It doesn't matter, darling,' Charlie reassured him. 'I'm not upset, really, just a bit melancholic. In a funny sort of way it's part of the healing.'

In spite of Matt's jacket around her shoulders, she shivered again. 'Brrrr, let's go,' she said.

★ ★ ★

'Do you like it?' Matt asked as Charlie tilted her hand this way and that to catch the light.

'It's beautiful!' she said in answer. It was a band of white gold set with two diamonds and an emerald.

'The green matches the colour of your eyes perfectly,' he said, raising her hand up to the side of her head.

'Emeralds have long been considered a token of constant love,' said the jeweller. 'Sacred to Venus, the goddess of love. It suits you, madam.'

'We'll take it,' said Matt.

'I want to buy you a ring, too,' Charlie reminded him.

'I have the very thing,' the jeweller suggested. 'It could be the masculine equivalent of that one for looks, actually. I'm afraid it's a little more pricey because it's heavier, though the stones aren't so big.'

'You can't,' Matt protested.

'Why not? Try it on,' Charlie urged him.

It fitted perfectly and Charlie was determined.

'I know . . . ' she said to the jeweller. 'Do you buy jewellery? I'd like to sell this wedding ring . . . part-exchange perhaps. It means nothing to me now . . . '

I loved Kent, truly I did, she told herself silently, *but every time I look at that ring now I think of cheating emails and credit card fraud and ending up paying for this ring myself, as well as all of Kent's other gifts to me.*

She slipped the wedding ring off her finger. *Time to move on*, she told herself.

'Yes, indeed I do. May I have a look, please?' The jeweller screwed a magnifying lens into his scrunched up eye and studied the ring carefully.

'Oh, yes, yes . . . I think we can come to some arrangement.' He took the lens from his eye and gave them a soft, sweet smile. 'Ah, young love,' he said. 'A perk of the job.'

★　★　★

'Let's invite your mum and dad over for a barbecue,' suggested Matt as he was stacking the dishwasher one evening.

Charlie shrugged non-committally.

'I don't think it's good that you're drifting apart from them,' Matt went on. 'I know they don't like me much, and certainly don't approve of us living together, but then, all they remember is the bleak time when you thought I'd abandoned you.

'They don't really know me at all. Let's face it, the only time they've seen me in the last five years was that painful encounter on the doorstep just after the tsunami, and when we moved the furniture and had the horrible row over Kent's clothes.'

'That's true, I suppose. I love Mum and Dad and I don't want to drift away from them really. They were upset when I moved in with you; they think it's far too early.' Charlie shrugged again and added, 'I don't suppose it occurred to them that living with them was driving me nuts. Perhaps we could invite Aunty Sophie and the girls as well . . . make a real party of it?'

'Later, maybe. One small step at a time, eh?'

'Actually, I think I'd rather have a lot of people over — safety in numbers,' she suggested. 'That'll dilute any angst and make people behave better. We could invite people from work, as well as your parents . . . '

'Isn't that just complicating things?'

'Why?'

'You know how your parents think my name is mud for dumping you without a word and then grabbing you on the rebound? Well, I'm afraid my parents are firmly convinced you're a shameless heartbreaker . . . '

Charlie burst out laughing.

'Perhaps it's best not to invite both sets at once then,' she agreed. 'Or they'll end up at each others' throats.'

Her laughter subsided and the two were silent for a moment before she asked, 'Perhaps we should show them the emails?'

'I'm not sure even that would convince them,' Matt sighed. 'They'd probably think we'd forged them just to explain away the past.'

'Okay, we'll just invite my parents then, and friends from my old team, a couple of neighbours perhaps.' Charlie turned a pleading look on Matt and shuddered. 'I'm not inviting just my parents on their own or it will be the Spanish Inquisition backed up by Aunty Sophie.

'Oh, I know they mean well and I love them to bits really, but they're so . . . so . . . *clucky* — and fixed in their opinions.'

Eventually, they agreed to set a date for the coming weekend because the weather forecast was good and everyone's duties meant they would be on rest days — a coincidence that didn't happen very often.

Charlie bought a cheap kettledrum barbecue because although she enjoyed barbecues she wasn't sure they would have them very often and a fancy barbecue would be a bit of an extravagance. Her dad had built a very fancy one at her mum and dad's house when barbecues were the 'thing' — all bricks, chimney and grids — and they probably used it once a year.

It was hard for Charlie to forget the panic she'd felt over Kent's debts. She'd probably be frugal for the rest of her days, she thought.

★ ★ ★

The warm June Saturday was perfect for the barbecue. There was no wind, so even the smoke behaved itself.

Charlie's mum and dad arrived first, shortly followed by Aunty Sophie and the girls. They'd brought some extra chairs with them and a fold-down picnic table, which was just as well because Charlie and Matt didn't have much garden furniture.

'Darling,' said Charlie's mum exuberantly, giving her a hug and a kiss, then looked nonplussed as to how to greet Matt.

He took the initiative and embraced

her with a kiss on the cheek, taking her by surprise, then shook hands with Charlie's dad in a stiff sort of way.

Aunty Sophie insisted on a tour of the house. 'I haven't seen it before,' she explained, 'Unlike your mum and dad.'

'I think Dad saw rather too much of it when he was renovating it,' quipped Charlie.

She showed her aunt upstairs first. 'The bathroom's just to your left, and there's the smallest bedroom — we're using that as a study . . . and this is the spare bedroom . . . and this one's mine — I mean ours.'

Aunty Sophie walked in and admired the décor before giving Charlie a speculative look. 'Are you happy?'

Charlie sighed. 'I know this will sound awful, but I'm the happiest I've been in years. I feel like my life is back on track the way it would have gone if Kent hadn't . . .

'Anyway, life's too short, I reckon. I hope I'll be happy — I think I'll be happy — but I refuse to hold back just because of a small risk that I might be unhappy.'

'Good for you my girl,' her aunt said, surprising Charlie just a little. 'I wish you all the best.'

More friends arrived, along with the people from next door and soon the party was under way, with the men giving Matt unnecessary helpful advice on how to get the best out of their little barbecue.

'I must build you a proper one,' threatened Charlie's dad.

Charlie's mum wanted to look at their new vegetable patch.

'One good thing about these old houses is that they come with decent sized gardens,' she said as Charlie took her down the garden path to the vegetable garden, past a lovely huge old camellia bush she had inherited when she bought the house.

'We haven't planted much, just sown a few salad things,' said Charlie. 'And I got a couple of courgette plants from the garden centre. Matt's been great at cutting the grass and stuff. He bought a new mower because the other one got nicked.'

Her mum bent down to pull up a dandelion and when she straightened she said quietly, 'He seems very nice. He's grown up a lot since I saw him last. I'm pleasantly surprised.'

'That was five years ago, Mum.' Charlie rolled her eyes. 'We've all grown up a lot since then.'

'Do you miss Kent?' Her mum twizzled the weed round in her fingers idly.

'Of course I do. I really did love him when I married him, but he's dead and I have to move on.'

Her mum crimped her lips together. 'I suppose it was inevitable with Matt waiting in the wings. I know you think I'm old-fashioned, but I can't help it; to me, he's leaped into your life with unseemly haste, and I don't like it. In Victorian times there were set periods of mourning, you know.'

Charlie burst out laughing.

'And in Victorian times children were shoved up chimneys or worked long hours in dark satanic mills!' she said. 'Look, Mum, I understand, really I do. It's just that I had a fright with Kent dying like that. Nobody seems to have given any thought to the fact that if it hadn't been for that court case meaning I had to stay in England, I would have been with him and I could easily have died out there, too.'

Her mother's eyes flashed wide and her hand flew to her throat. 'Oh, don't say things like that.'

'But it's true, Mum,' Charlie said. 'I've had to face my own mortality and I'm not going to put off things I want to do until some unspecified time in the future — in case there isn't one.'

'I know darling. I understand, really I do. I just want what's best for you,' she said as she hugged Charlie.

As evening fell people left one by one until Charlie and Matt were just left with the glowing embers and good memories.

The evening was drifting into a balmy night. The roses, which had been wilting under the blazing sun, perked up and their scent grew heavy in the night air. White flowers picked out the last of the evening light.

Charlie was in Matt's arms, sitting on the swinging hammock seat. He was rocking them both gently, lips pressed to her head, his breath a blessing over her hair.

'Happy?' he asked.

'Perfectly,' said Charlie.

★ ★ ★

A few days later, Charlie told Matt, 'I really enjoyed that barbecue. I like entertaining people and we should do it more often. I was thinking we should invite DI Benton and her hubby over for dinner one evening. She's been a real brick to me over the last few months.'

'You brown-noser,' Matt teased.

Charlie gave him a mock-glare and

stuck her tongue out. Oh, he did look handsome with that quirky grin of his! 'No, seriously, she's not just a great Inspector, she's been a good listener. I'd like to thank her.'

'I bet she won't come.'

As it happened, she did. She said to call her Kaye off duty, but Charlie couldn't help calling her 'ma'am' most of the evening, which made them all laugh.

Kaye's husband, Richard, was an interesting bloke. He was also a copper but in a different division. They had two kids who were grown up and had left home.

'Did you find it easy when they were small, ma'am — I mean, Kaye?' Charlie asked.

'Not really. We worked shifts which was okay for looking after the kids but we hardly saw each other. And we were lucky since Richard's parents were close enough to babysit if exigencies of duty delayed us unexpectedly. It was tough at times but it was worth it — they're great kids.' DI Benton gave a soft smile.

Everyone retreated to the living room over coffee — delicious real coffee which Charlie had taken a recent liking to. The three piece suite that she thought she'd never be able to bear sitting on again was fine in this setting, out of the context of her home in married quarters. Charlie ran a hand over it, thinking *It's been hard, but I really think I'm moving on now.*

She stood, poured more coffee and was just about to make a remark along those lines and thank DI Benton for her help and support when the doorbell rang. Matt went to answer it, but Charlie said, 'No, I'll get it, I'm on my feet already.'

The doorbell rang again, aggressively, insistently, and there was hammering on the wood. Charlie could see the bulk of a figure moving outside through the frosted glass. It must be an emergency, she thought, reaching for the doorknob. 'I'm coming, give us a chance,' she called, opening the door wide.

Kent.

All the blood drained from Charlie's face and her legs gave way; she would have fallen had Matt not caught her.

'I see you didn't waste any time climbing into my bed,' Kent snarled, swinging a punch at Matt, but missing as Matt dodged. Charlie tried to regain her legs but Kent pushed her roughly and she sagged deeper into Matt's arms as Kent tried to barge into the hallway.

Matt slid round sideways and landed a foot in Kent's midriff, forcing him back out of the door. 'Run, Kent, run. I broke into your computer and I know all about your fraud and so do the police. They're after you, Kent, you're a wanted man.'

Charlie heard running footsteps behind her and DI Benton's voice shouting, 'Let us through! Kent Henley, I'm arresting you on suspicion of . . .'

Kent blanched, turned and fled, vaulting over the gate. They heard a car start up, a horrible crunch of gears, then the roar of the car speeding away.

'Keys and phone, c'mon,' said Richard. 'Go, go, go!'

Charlie slithered aside as Kaye and Richard ran out the house for their car, Richard already on his mobile.

'Don't worry, I used to be a traffic rat,' yelled Kaye as they jumped into their car.

'Come in and lock the door, we're not out of the woods yet,' said Matt anxiously. 'You okay?'

'That's her personal car, she's not insured for pursuit in that,' was all Charlie could think to say.

'I imagine she'll just try and keep up with him, see where he goes until proper pursuit cars will take over. Oh, my love, here . . . ' Matt held out a hand and helped Charlie to her feet.

'He's alive. Trev was wrong . . . ' she said in wonderment.

'You're shaking, come and sit down.' Matt hugged her close.

They staggered into the living room and Charlie flopped onto the sofa, limp and shattered. 'I don't believe it, I just don't believe it . . . it was Kent, wasn't it?'

Matt looked furious. 'I can't believe it, either. I wonder why he's only just turned up?' He looked down at Charlie. 'Are you sure you're okay? Did he hurt you when he shoved you?'

'No, I'm all right. I've had far worse on duty. You said you knew all about him and his fraud . . . what did you mean, Matt?'

'That was sheer bluff. I wasn't in a position to defend you, holding you in my arms like that. I wanted to make him run, leave us alone. I didn't want to have to fight him, though I would have if he'd forced me to.'

'Fine copper I make, fainting like that . . . sorry . . . '

'You'd just had the most massive shock; anyone would have fainted — I nearly did! That's why he caught me out.'

There was a sound of a car drawing up. Matt froze and went to the window. Charlie's heart was racing as she stood ready in case Kent broke in.

'It's Kaye and Richard. They must have lost him,' Matt said and went to open the door.

'We backed off as soon as the pursuit vehicles took over. The helicopter's above him now, so it's really only a matter of time. How badly hurt are you both?'

'I'm okay,' they both said at once just as another vehicle drew up — a police car.

'I expect we'll have to do statements,' Matt said.

'You're going to have to do more than statements, I'm afraid,' said Kaye. 'This is far, far more serious than that. You're both going to have to be interviewed under caution.'

DI Benton sighed heavily and went on, 'Charlie, you'll need a Fed rep and solicitor, and Matt, you should have a rep from your union and a solicitor.'

Charlie realised with a cold twist of her heart that this was serious. The Police Federation was like a union for police ranks below Chief Inspector. They supplied a Fed Friend and solicitor in disciplinary cases or when a police officer was accused of a criminal offence. She turned her anxious eyes to Matt. He looked just as puzzled as she felt.

'Don't worry,' DI Benton said, 'I'll sort that side of things out for you, but I can't be involved with your interviews; I'm a witness now, you see, and I've been doing the investigation.'

'Are we under arrest?' asked Matt. 'What investigation?'

'No, you're not under arrest at the moment; you're going to do a voluntary interview under caution at the police station,' DI Benton explained. 'Which means that anything you do say might be used as evidence if we then think you've committed an offence. In theory you could walk out and it won't be held against you. But . . . well, speak to the solicitor, he or she will advise you. I shouldn't say anything more — and neither should you at present.'

'But I was defending Charlie, I had to kick him, and it was a shove more than a kick,' Matt said indignantly.

'Say nothing until you have a solicitor with you for advice,' said Kaye. 'Sorry, but you'll have to go in separate police cars to separate police stations, and Professional Standards will take over from there.'

Charlie's heart sank. Professional Standards? Serious disciplinary offences were suspected of herself and Matt, then, or even something criminal. But what?

11

'Goodbye, and thanks,' Charlie said as she got out of the police car. Dawn was breaking and she felt as mangled as a well-wrung flannel when she unlocked her front door.

Matt rushed into the hall the second she stepped across the threshold. 'Oh, thank goodness! I was worried it might be Kent.' He grabbed her, hugged her tight.

'He's been arrested. Didn't they tell you? His fingerprints check out against the ones taken when he was arrested for D&D so they knew for sure it's him. He's changed a lot, lost weight, but when they showed me a photo of course I knew him . . . oh, you didn't know about the drunk and disorderly?'

'No . . . yes . . . but still. I'm a bit jumpy . . . not thinking straight, that's all. What happened? I'm still really,

really confused.'

'I want a decent coffee and a shower, then we'll talk.'

Charlie scrubbed herself from head to foot, then threw on some fluffy pyjamas. It was July, already hot outside, but she felt cold to the marrow.

Matt had the coffee ready when she came down. 'What happened?' he said as he poured her one.

'You first,' she said as if trying to avoid the inevitable.

'They just asked about Christmas time and the days following the tsunami. And they asked me to pick out Kent and Trev from a load of photographs. I knew who Kent was but not Trev. They asked me if I'd heard from either of them since the tsunami and I told them just that phone call and the email, and I said they could take the computers when they dropped me off. I hope you don't mind . . . ' Matt looked distraught.

'No, you did the right thing. We should be in the clear, but I can see what they're thinking . . . '

'What?'

'Think about it, Matt,' Charlie sighed. 'Kent's up to his eyeballs in debt, debt I'm apparently party to and liable for after he moved the debt to another joint card. He disappears, supposedly dead from the tsunami, and I claim on his life insurance and pay off those debts . . . but he's not dead, just purporting to be someone else.'

'Who?'

'Trev, as far as I can gather.'

'You mean it was Kent who phoned from Bangkok, Kent who sent that email, not Trev?' Matt sat back on the sofa, flicked his hair back with a perplexed rake with his fingers. 'I don't believe it. I thought Trev had made a mistake.'

'Looks like it, reading between the lines. But look, Matt, I don't know for sure because they didn't tell me this, I'm just guessing. Trev and Kent have a passing resemblance — I saw it in the church as we got married — though

Trev's stockier and a bit older. How hard would it be for Kent to assume Trev's identity, ID Trev's body as himself, have him conveniently buried in a mass grave? Then he could assume Trev's identity, apart from his job, which he abandoned by sending an email.'

'Not that easy, surely?' Matt was silent for a few minutes. 'It all fits, though — like the way Trev stopped posting on that forum . . . the way nobody saw him . . . even the way he sold the house. But I still don't understand why he did it. Okay, there were the debts but . . . surely he couldn't bear to do that to you? I thought he loved you . . . '

'It wasn't just the debts, though, Matt,' Charlie reasoned. 'I think Kent was suffering from Post Traumatic Stress Disorder from his time in Iraq, and it was getting worse. I begged him to get help but instead he took the opportunity when it arose to desert so he wouldn't have to go back on active service. Something awful happened in Iraq, Matt — a good mate was horribly killed when he might have been okay if Kent had been a bit braver, and it's unmanned him . . . I thought I'd told you.'

'You did . . . Simbo.'

'Yes. As for what he put me through . . . I thought he loved me too, but now I think he just saw me as a trophy to win from you. It was cruel, Matt, to do that to me — and to his parents . . . ' Charlie sighed heavily but then looked up at Matt with her chin tilted defiantly. 'I'm going to divorce him for unreasonable behaviour. Then you and I can get married properly.'

'Oh my love!' said Matt, throwing himself at her and hugging her close. She could feel his heart pounding against hers and he was shaking slightly. 'I love you so much . . . to think I thought him a friend all those years.'

'I know, love, I know.' Charlie raised her face and Matt covered it with kisses.

Resigned, Charlie sat back and sipped her coffee in silence for a moment. 'They asked me the same sorts of questions as they asked you, and whether I'd been aware of Kent's financial problems. I said no, of course. If I had been, perhaps I'd have had warning bells about him and not married him. Perhaps he thought I was wealthy and would be able to bail him out. Of course the signature on the joint credit card thing is a bit damning, but I told them it was forged. Luckily I'd already told DI Benton about that.'

'So what now?' he asked. 'I'm suspended. I hate that, it makes me feel like a criminal.'

She bit her lip. 'Me too. The thing is, though, Matt, the police have to be careful because, for all they know I could be involved, could be play-acting . . . I could have been in cahoots with Kent about all this all along. It looks really dodgy — and you know what really makes me go cold? If it weren't for you, I might have been here on my own when Kent appeared out of the blue like that and it would have been a lot harder to argue that I didn't know and that I'm not involved with his fraud.'

'So you think the police are happy that we're not involved, then?' Matt looked anxious, and Charlie yearned to stroke his hair from his eyes.

'More like they haven't found any evidence that we are involved — and that's not quite the same.'

'So that's why we're suspended? How long for?'

'Who knows?' she said ruefully.

'Will we have to pay the insurance money back?'

Charlie swore. 'Yes, I think we will — and I can't afford it. Don't tell me I'll have to sell the house after all . . . '

'It's Kent's debt, let him deal with it,' Matt said sharply.

'But it's not, is it? I used the life insurance to clear his debts, yes, but the insurance was paid out to me, so it's me who'll have to pay it back.'

'I think we should take legal advice on it, especially as he obtained the card fraudulently. Why not phone your Fed solicitor and see what he says?'

'I don't know. It's not exactly a Fed matter, is it?'

Matt sighed and buried his head in his hands. 'It might be . . . you can only ask. I'm too tired and muddled to think this through properly. I think the best thing is to wait and see what happens, see if the Insurance company wants it back, see what happens about Kent. I have to admit I hope he goes to jail, because he scares me.' Matt shuddered.

'I suppose I could argue that the life insurance is Kent's problem, but it's hanging over me. If I had the money I'd pay it back just to feel better about it. I hate being in debt, even if it's not mine.' Charlie bit her lip. Debt was anathema to her, and even if she weren't legally responsible — she would have to find that out — she felt morally responsible. 'And besides, the police service takes a dim view of unmanaged debt.'

'Try not to worry about it. I know it's morning, but I'm going to bed — I'm shattered. Things might look better later on.'

★   ★   ★

Charlie woke, dressed quietly so as not to disturb Matt, made herself a coffee and went to sit in the garden on the hammock. She rocked herself idly letting her thoughts drift as she tried to make sense of it all, but it was no good — everywhere she looked everything was up in the air, and all decisions depended on other people.

Suspended. Still, at least it was on full pay.

Normally she enjoyed rest days and annual leave, even if she didn't do anything more than potter round the garden, but this felt all wrong, somehow.

The one constant was Matt, her beloved Matt.

And at least DI Benton had seen her reaction when Kent appeared on the doorstep. That should surely make her believe that she wasn't involved.

On the other hand, how simple would it be to stage the whole thing by inviting her boss over for dinner, and then effectively blocking the gangway when Kent appeared? No — scrap that idea because Kent had been caught, and how would he gain anything by showing himself like that? By calling round, he had given his game away.

Where had he been for the last six months? He must have been in this country to sell Trev's house — and who witnessed his signature on the contract? Perhaps he'd bribed them to witness under false names. This was serious fraud, and Kent was deep in the brown sticky stuff. What a fool!

A Jenny wren was busy in the undergrowth and a robin was bragging in a tree. The summer scents soothed Charlie as she rocked and mulled things over.

'Hello, love,' said Matt. 'I wondered where you were.' He sat down next to her.

'It was too perfect, you know . . . I was too happy . . . '

'We'll get through it somehow, love. We've got through some awful stuff before now,' he replied reassuringly. 'I think we might as well make the best of our time off. Let's finish getting the garden sorted or do some decorating or paint the shed,' he suggested. 'We can go for walks, days by the seaside, stuff like that. We've done nothing wrong, Charlie, and we've got nothing to be ashamed of.'

Charlie nestled her head on his shoulder. 'I love you, Matt. You're so positive. And you're right, it's a lovely day. Let's dig the rest of that veggie patch like we've been meaning to . . . and weed the beds, get on top of it after those tenants let it go to pot.'

★　★　★

Next day they decided to go shopping for plants and sort out a family law solicitor for Charlie's divorce. Charlie was locking the front door when Matt grabbed her and kissed her.

'Love you,' he said before they got in the car and drove off.

'I want one of everything!' Charlie joked when they got to the garden centre.

'Me too, but we'd better not spend too much, love, not if . . . '

Charlie felt a finger of ice run down her spine. 'True,' she conceded bleakly. 'Still, it's nice to look.'

They spent a couple of hours looking round and in the end only bought a handful of plants, but to Charlie that didn't matter because she'd had a pleasant morning with the man she loved.

The next day it was raining fitfully and too miserable to enjoy working in the garden so Charlie suggested, 'How about going to town? We could have a mooch round the museum, or the charity shops . . . I could do with some more books and I don't want to buy new if we're being careful with the pennies.'

'Great idea,' Matt agreed.

As they got in the car, Matt said, 'That car was here yesterday, that one with the shifty-looking man with his window wound down. Perhaps we should phone the local neighbourhood policing officer?'

'I'll make a note of his index,' said Charlie, fishing out a notebook and taking down the number plate.

They parked in the supermarket car park, intending to look round town first, then do their shopping for groceries.

'Did you see that?' asked Charlie as they walked to the high street. 'Or am I being paranoid?'

'What?'

'People keep looking at us . . . you know, on the sly, out of the corner of their eyes. It's creeping me out a bit.'

'I hadn't noticed,' Matt replied, but a

little further he said, 'Yes, now you mention it, people are staring . . . looking, then looking away quickly, but watching us from the corner of their eyes as we pass. I swear I saw someone nudge the person they were with and whisper something.'

They tried to convince each other that they were just being paranoid, but the same happened in the charity shop.

Charlie was scanning the books with that cricked-neck stance peculiar to people reading book titles on the spines, when someone bumped into her, said, 'Sorry,' then did a double take and moved away.

Charlie selected a few novels and when she paid, the woman at the till gave her a long stare. 'Do I know you from somewhere?' the woman asked.

'Not unless I've had cause to arrest you in the past,' Charlie replied somewhat acidly, then smiled to take the sting from her words. 'Which is rather unlikely, don't you think?'

They both laughed, but Charlie felt

the woman's gaze on her back as she and Matt left the shop. *Stop it! That really is being paranoid,* she told herself.

Then, in the supermarket, they saw the papers.

On the front page of the tabloids were pictures of Kent, herself and Matt.

'What the . . . ' said Matt. He picked one up, one renowned for its lurid headlines, and scanned it quickly. It had a photograph of Charlie and Matt kissing on the doorstep.

He swore under his breath. 'I think we'd better get some supplies in, love. I have the feeling we may find ourselves under siege.' He put a copy of every newspaper into the trolley, and they went round again buying extra supplies of milk and bread, just in case. 'What's in the freezer?' he asked.

'We have plenty,' said Charlie. She could feel her heart racing, her fists clenching involuntarily.

At the checkout the cashier kept looking at them, and when the papers went through last, she looked about to say something but thought better of it.

Charlie could feel heat on her face as they slipped out of the door and back to the car park. 'I don't think I can face ever shopping there again,' she said.

They walked briskly to the car and loaded it up.

'If that man's still there in his car, I've a good mind to give him what for,' Matt said crossly. 'This is an invasion of our privacy, you know.'

'Don't,' warned Charlie. 'That newspaper is renowned for its hatred of the police and you'll only give them something to quote if you do.'

When they got there the car with its sinister occupant had been joined by several others and one of their neighbours was talking to someone.

Matt muttered something rude as he parked, then they got out and rushed the shopping inside.

'I'm just going to check the garden gate's locked,' said Matt.

Charlie drew the curtains closed,

then put the kettle on. 'They'll get bored and leave us alone when the next scandal hits the headlines. Don't let it faze you,' she said as Matt stomped back indoors.

She hefted the pile of newspapers onto the table beside their coffee mugs and said, 'Let's look at the damage, shall we?'

* ★ *

Most concentrated on Kent's story: *Soldier Back From The Dead*, or *Tsunami Victim's Double Life*, even *AWOL Cheat Soldier Charged*.

'Oh,' said Matt. 'Looks like he's been charged with something . . . yes, fraud, deception . . . and he'll have to face a court martial for desertion, too. Serves him right.'

Charlie shook her head sadly.

'It does, love,' Matt insisted. 'Look what he's done to us. Split us up with hurtful fraudulent emails, married you when he was deep in debt and made you responsible by fraudulently forging your signature, assumed Trev's identity, leading you to believe he was dead, deserted his regiment, and then came back here and tried to bully his way back into your life.'

'I know . . . but I can't help feeling a lot of it was due to Post-Traumatic Stress Disorder.'

'No, love, he wasn't suffering that when he sent those emails to split us up. That was just plain wicked.'

'True.' Charlie picked up one of the papers. 'But we were young and immature then.'

Tsunami Scumbag Soldier, went the headline. *When thousands lost their lives in the biggest ever natural disaster of the modern age, including best friend Trevor Hardwick, soldier Kent Henley assumed his dead friend's identity to avoid fighting in Iraq, even though that meant abandoning his wife of three months and childhood sweetheart, Charlotte. But love rat Charlotte, and her lover Martin Pennington,*

couldn't wait to spend the life insur-
ance money on new furniture for her
£230,000 house in Galenbury where
they now live as man and wife. It's
understood from a source we cannot
reveal that they were also arrested on
suspicion of fraud, but later released
without charge.

'What rubbish, that's just not true!' said Charlie angrily. 'They can't even get your name right. Matt Penningby, not Martin Pennington. They must have been talking with a neighbour who saw us moving the new stuff in and then going off in the squad car. And what they don't know they simply invent. And why do they have to tell people the value of our home? What business is it of theirs?'

'Sue-with-the-Leylandii wouldn't do that, would she?'

'No, not her. She's keen on privacy, and besides, she knows that wasn't new furniture we brought in. Someone else, then. Someone we don't know that well, a curtain twitcher perhaps.'

'Love rat'. I've a good mind to shove this paper where the sun don't shine,' said Matt savagely. 'Should we sue them?'

'That would be expensive and they can afford the kind of slippery lawyers that we can't, especially if divorcing Kent is going to cost so much,' Charlie said, resignedly flicking the pages. 'I'm angry and I would like to get them back for this,' she agreed, 'but we can't. Trashy papers like this often publish one-sided stories solely from the viewpoint of the story: the poor 'innocent victim' of police brutality. In reality he's actually some drunkard who's refused a breath test and has been stroppy, violent and vile-mouthed all the way to the nick and in custody. But of course, that side of the story never gets published, not even when the officer is exonerated.'

Charlie sighed. 'I'm afraid we just have to take it on the chin. Coppers always do, you know.'

Matt sat glowering for several minutes, then he jumped up. 'I'm going to take photographs of them — and get my telescope out. Just for the fun of it.'

'What good will that do?'

'No good at all, I suppose, but it'll make me feel better.'

'I hope they don't keep this up for long,' Charlie groaned. 'It's going to drive me nuts.'

Matt came back downstairs a few minutes later. 'Come upstairs a minute, love. I want to show you something.'

Charlie followed him into the front bedroom where the curtains were drawn except for a tiny crack. 'Have a look at that scumbag reporter's car; can you see him in it?'

Charlie looked hard. 'Not unless he's lying down, no.'

'Right, come into the back bedroom, don't go close to the windows but look in the old camellia bush.'

At first Charlie saw nothing, but then she caught a glimpse of movement and the swift flash of sunlight on a lens. 'The cheeky monkey!' she said. 'How did he get into the back garden?'

'Over the fence, I imagine. It's only six foot — and not everyone locks their gate; he could have come over a neighbour's fence.' Matt suddenly looked very mischievous. 'I think it's time to water the garden, don't you?'

'We have every right to water our garden. Let's do it!' Charlie said, then added, 'But look, I'll go outside first, distract him and make it hard for him to slip back over the fence without showing himself. Then you get the hosepipe out and start watering the beds and get closer to the camellia bush. When you start on that, if he sits there and takes it, I'll start chatting and you keep spraying as if distracted.' Charlie grinned. 'We must make it look accidental.'

'I think we should feed the garden too . . . ' Matt suggested. 'We could put some of that awful stinky comfrey concentrate you've been making in that diluter thing that fits on the hose.'

Charlie wandered out into the garden carrying a pair of secateurs. She was

239

wearing a baseball cap and sunglasses. 'It's hot out here still,' she called to Matt, then wandered further up the garden and started deadheading a rose, facing the camellia bush. She took her time and Matt had plenty of time to get the hose out. She saw him decant some of the horribly stinky liquid feed into a diluter that attached to the hose. It was made from decomposing comfrey leaves and reputed to be an excellent plant tonic. Matt started watering, casually working his way up the garden.

'Can you give that one a good feed?' Charlie said innocently. 'Its leaves are going yellow and that means it's hungry.'

Matt played the hose onto the camellia bush. Charlie thought she heard a sudden intake of breath. 'Give it a good soak please, love, and then do the rest of the garden.'

'Okay, love.'

'It's terrible being a prisoner in our own home, isn't it?'

'Yes, I do hate those newspaper

vultures, don't you?'

'They tell such lies. I wonder if they'd like us to dig out some dirt on some of them,' said Charlie, trying hard to keep her face serious. 'I bet some of them have criminal records.'

'The way some of them behave, I can believe it.'

'Come round this side, you've missed a bit. The best way to water is to give things a really good soaking once in a while.'

Once they'd got the hose out it seemed sensible to give the whole garden a good watering anyway. The camellia bush hadn't shaken once and Charlie wondered if they were too late and perhaps their quarry had vanished as they came downstairs.

'Mind the wasps' nest,' said Charlie casually.

Matt gave her a quizzical look, so she winked. 'Which one?' he asked, cottoning on.

'The one by the fence near the camellia bush. I forgot to say earlier;

they won't like being flooded out!'

Back inside the house they both laughed at each other, but when Charlie sobered up she said, 'I hope that wasn't unwise. He could do us a lot of damage by lying about us in the papers. It's hard to undo any damage the papers do, even if they're shown to be libellous. Their apologies are usually a couple of lines buried in the middle of the paper.'

As it was, a couple of days later the media siege was lifted, presumably because it was now old news.

12

'I'm thinking of installing CCTV in the garden, front and back, and an intercom on the door,' said Matt. He was sprawled on the sofa with his head on Charlie's lap while she was idly stroking his hair.

'Why? I think the media have lost interest in us.'

'I was thinking, suppose Kent gets let out on bail? I don't want him coming here bent on vengeance.'

'He won't come here, I don't think. And I'm not sure about bail because I know how perverse courts can be. I wish I knew what was going on, and I'm bored with being suspended.'

'I'm not bored so much as humiliated, but it has its plus points,' said Matt pulling her down for a kiss.

* * *

'That blasted reporter is outside again,' said Matt a few days later. 'What does he want now?'

'Slow news day? Or perhaps there's news about Kent and he wants a story,' Charlie suggested.

They'd just made coffee when the doorbell rang. Charlie looked through the spy hole before opening the front door. 'Oh, it's you, ma'am. Come in.'

DI Benton stepped into the hall. Charlie wasn't quite sure how to greet her, so in the end she just said, 'Would you like to come through?' and led her into the living room.

DI Benton's face gave nothing away. 'Please sit down,' Charlie suggested and when DI Benton seated herself, Charlie and Matt sat down too, perching nervously on the edge of the sofa. 'Is there news, ma'am?'

'Yes, there is,' she said finally. 'We can find no credible evidence of your involvement in the fraud, so no charges will be brought against you, and we're returning your computers. I have them in the car.'

'What a relief! And I've missed my computer,' said Matt.

Charlie felt like kissing DI Benton. 'Does this mean our suspensions are lifted then?'

'Can't wait to get back to work?' DI Benton had an amused gleam in her eye. 'You can come back on Monday. Kent has pleaded guilty to all charges, which means we won't need you as witnesses either. It's now just a matter of his sentencing and then passing him to his regiment for court martial.'

'Probably a year, suspended,' said Charlie, only half in jest.

'Tsk, tsk, so cynical for one so young,' DI Benton said.

'I'm a copper; cynicism goes with the job. What's the story, please, ma'am? We've been trying to guess but we've only read what's in the papers, and you know what they do to news.'

'Is that coffee I can smell?' hinted DI Benton.

Matt started up from the sofa. 'Yes,

just made. I'll bring it through here.'

'It's like this,' said DI Benton when the coffee was poured. 'You remember when you had your little heart-to-heart with me, Charlie, when you told me what had happened and your doubts and how betrayed you felt that Trev hadn't even bothered to come and see you about Kent's death?

'Now, I met Trev at your wedding and I had a long chat with him and he struck me as a very nice young man,' she went on. 'So that kind of callous behaviour seemed out of character. I could understand the frantic phone call when he was still in Bangkok, but I was pretty sure he would have made contact with you when he got back in England.

'I asked to look at your wedding photos because I wanted to be sure I was thinking of the right young man . . . ' She looked at Charlie and Matt in turn. 'Have you noticed how similar Trev and Kent look?'

'Yes, I have actually,' Charlie replied.

'Then you told me Trev's house was

sold when you went to see if you could find him to get him to be a witness at the inquest and that seemed odd to me, too. Of course, it could just have been that he was disturbed by the experience and wanted to make a new start somewhere else.'

DI Benton put her cup on the table. 'But altogether the story started ringing alarm bells. I thought how easy it would be to deliberately and fraudulently misidentify someone in all that chaos, during such a terrible, harrowing time. So Kent, whom you told me you believed to be suffering from Post Traumatic Stress Disorder — or shell shock as it was called years ago — and who owed thousands on his credit cards, was conveniently dead.' DI Benton shrugged. 'And in his place was Trev, newly out of the army, reasonably well off, and better still, with no living close relatives except an aunt, uncle and cousins conveniently a long way away. Very neat,' she said.

'Then you told me of Kent's

despicable behaviour with the fraudulent emails when you were kids,' she continued, 'and how he'd forged your signature on the credit card transfer a few months ago, making you jointly liable, in order to increase his credit limit. So he had 'previous' for fraud, albeit unproven . . .

'Now, do you remember who signed the register at your wedding?' she asked Charlie.

'Trev and Aunty Sophie.'

'And who autographed your wedding photo album?'

'The bridesmaids and best man . . . Trev again.'

'I went to see the firm who did the conveyancing for the sale of Trev's house,' DI Benton told them. 'The contracts looked all above board, witnessed and everything. But Trev's signature, though very similar, really wasn't the same — and, as it turned out, the witnesses were not the people they said they were.'

Charlie and Matt looked at each

other as their suspicions were confirmed and DI Benton continued her story.

'This was enough evidence for me to get a warrant to look at Trev's bank accounts and, unlike everything else, those have been active . . . let's just say that over the last six months the amount of money he had in those accounts dwindled to practically nothing, and it had been quite a substantial amount, what with the house sale and all. I hate to think what Kent's been spending it on.'

'So he thought he'd come back to me secretly,' Charlie gasped incredulously. 'He just assumed I was languishing as a mournful and loving widow who would be delighted to have him back and go along with his scam?'

'Yes, I'm afraid he did,' DI Benton sighed. 'He admitted as much to us. He said it was a shock to find Matt here with you — even more of a shock when Matt said he'd broken into his computer and that we were after him.

'Ironically, Matt didn't know it, but we *were* after him. Kent had been driving Trev's car round on Trev's insurance, spending Trev's money . . . we had him logged as 'wanted' and if he'd driven past an ANPR camera, it would have pinged and we'd have got him then.'

DI Benton looked at Charlie and said warily, 'I didn't tell you, Charlie, because I wasn't completely certain it was only Kent who had done it.'

She flushed slightly and justified herself with, 'It seemed such a wickedly callous thing to do to you, that I admit I did wonder if you were all involved, some sort of menage a trois. I'm sorry to say we had to treat you both as suspects, especially as you'd used the life insurance to pay off the debts, Charlie,' she said sympathetically. 'Debts you appeared to have taken on when you signed the joint credit card application — the signature was near perfect, exactly like yours. In my heart I was convinced you were innocent, but if you're a copper you have to listen to your head, not your heart . . .

'Except where romance is concerned, of course,' DI Benton finished with a smile.

'I'm divorcing him, ma'am.' Charlie blushed. 'Then me and Matt can get married and . . . '

DI Benton smiled. 'When?'

'It seems to be taking ages, even though the lawyer assured me it would be a quickie.'

DI Benton burst out laughing. 'That sounds so dodgy!' she said. 'Well, I hope it all goes well for you and I'll see you Monday, then.' She rose from the sofa and walked towards the hallway, then turned. 'Oh, by the way, I saw off that nasty sneaky reporter for you.'

'Did you ma'am — how?' Charlie grinned.

'I recognised him from a little peccadillo a few years ago,' she replied. 'And as I like to remind my customers of my exceedingly long memory, I rapped on his car window for a little social chit-chat.' DI Benton smiled broadly. 'There was a very peculiar odour in his car . . . I said it smelled like cannabis, but he insisted it was some sort of fertiliser that he'd picked up from somewhere that had sunk into the fabric of his car seat. I told it really did smell like cannabis, but as I wasn't on duty I wouldn't search him, but that if he persisted in parking there other officers would know where to find him.'

DI Benton reached for the front door handle. 'He left pretty sharpish, I can tell you, which makes me wonder what he was hiding. I wonder what the smell was? It was only faint, but . . . phew!' She pulled a face and then said her goodbyes.

★　★　★

'Yes!' Matt cried out once DI Benton had gone, punching the air in victory. 'Oh, Charlie,' he added when she didn't cheer as well. 'Aren't you happy?'

'No, not really . . . ' Charlie sighed. 'I'm relieved, mostly . . . relieved that part is over, relieved we won't have to go to court, relieved that I'll soon be free to marry you . . . ' She gave Matt a thin smile. 'But a huge part of me is very sad about Kent. I keep thinking back to when we were cadets . . . we were the three musketeers, such good mates . . . but then we grew up and it all went wrong somehow.'

Matt pulled Charlie to her feet and hugged her.

'We can't go back, love; we can't change things,' he told her softly. 'Kent made his choices and they were bad ones, and his bad-choices have hurt you. His jealousy hurt all three of us. Perhaps his Post Traumatic Stress Disorder made him worse, but not everyone who is jealous or is stressed does such wicked things. So many people died in the tsunami, so many never came home, and he polluted the horror of it for his own ends. I feel sad but I think that's mainly because I thought I knew him, but really, I never knew him at all.'

13

'I'm off into town to get my hair done,' Charlie announced when she brought up a morning cup of tea for Matt. She sat on the edge of his bed. 'That's if I can get an appointment,' she added. 'I wish I'd thought to do it last week. I suppose I was getting used to being suspended.'

Matt sat himself up. 'Hello gorgeous,' he said and took the cup from Charlie.

'That usually sounds corny but from you it sounds just right.'

'That's because I mean it.' Matt smiled. 'Can't we hurry the divorce along a bit?'

'These things take time, I suppose. They told me it's progressing as fast as it can.'

'I know, love, I know . . . I'm just feeling impatient and grumpy . . . restless. I suppose I'm still riled that I was suspended,' he said. 'It made me feel like they assumed I'm was criminal. It was insulting.'

'I know, but they had to do it. And for me I don't suppose it will be the first time. I stand a good chance of ending up in the dock myself — albeit more so when I was on Response — to justify the level of force used against someone who really, really doesn't want to be nicked.'

'Why do you do it, love?' Matt asked, concerned. 'I have to admit, it's much better dealing with computers — at least they don't fight back!'

'I just love it, you know that,' she replied with a shrug. 'I can't explain it, really . . . I love protecting people from swindlers and con artists, I love being able to grab ill-gotten gains back from drug dealers, trying to right wrongs, I suppose . . . It's ironic that I happened to marry a fraud, isn't it?'

Matt felt it better to leave her to her thoughts, but was happy that she was getting out and about again. 'Well, have your girly day out if you insist,' he said, 'But I'm staying home.'

When Charlie stepped out of the front door she wondered if Matt had the right idea after all, as she was immediately pounced on by a number of reporters. *Oh no*, she groaned inwardly as she pushed through them, *why the sudden resurgence of interest?*

When she got to the hairdresser, her stylist started to chat as usual, but Charlie was barely responsive. She stared at herself in the mirror, seeing her usual cut emerge from the shaggy lengths she'd let it grow to.

She wasn't sure she liked sitting there, seeing herself staring back out of the mirror. Such a long, frank scrutiny was just too revealing of flaws. She saw a tired face, a drawn face, one with a firmer cast than before. She'd aged, she decided, that's what it was, and she no longer had those childish curves to her cheeks. With a jolt, she realised that it was no longer a girl's face looking back at her, but a woman's . . . and a beautiful woman's face at that.

Kent's plea of guilty was in the papers — that at least explained the reporters, she thought as she had to run the gauntlet when she got home. And Matt was in a funny mood, too, but she put it down to the reporters and forgot about it.

★ ★ ★

When they got to the Big House on Monday morning, it was as if the last few weeks' suspension had never happened, for Charlie at least. Glancing across at Matt, she wasn't so sure he felt the same way.

He had a slight flush and a tight step, not at all relaxed. Maybe this had humiliated him even more than he'd let on.

It dampened her mood such that, by the time she reached her team's office and Matt had gone on his department, she felt rather diffident. Everyone greeted her with guarded smiles and the first thing DI Benton did was to call her into her room and shut the door.

'Sit down, Charlie. You seen this?' DI Benton thrust a newpaper towards Charlie.

'No ma'am.' Charlie picked it up with a sinking feeling and read the headline.

Exclusive: My Life with Tsunami Soldier Fraud, it read.

'What? The swine!' Charlie skimmed down the article. 'I don't believe it! Where did they get all this from?'

'Where indeed,' DI Benton said slowly in a cold, dry tone. 'You do realise talking to journalists and telling them prurient stuff like this is acting in a manner likely to bring the service into disrepute — a serious disciplinary offence? By talking to the paper like this you've let me, the team and the force down — and more importantly, you've let yourself down.'

'But I didn't!' Charlie protested. 'They must have dug it up from somewhere else — neighbours, maybe

Kent's pals in the army — and stitched it all together to make a story.'

'Read it carefully, Charlie,' DI Benton said firmly. 'Look at the details they have, details I thought you'd kept private, and then try to tell me you didn't talk to this reporter.'

Charlie took the proffered paper and read through the article. It was written as if she had told the story, and included talk of when she, Matt and Kent were cadets.

It described her marriage, her brief months on the base, her anguish when Kent was reported dead by Trev, followed by her new life with Matt. There were details that only those who knew her well could know . . . and most damning of all was the revelation about the forged emails.

'I don't understand how they found all that out, unless the neighbours overheard us talking . . . ' Charlie was thinking out loud, trying to find and answer to it all. 'But we don't normally hear the people from next door, even

260

though it's a semi. I did see the people from next door talking to this paper's reporter, though . . . you know him, ma'am. You saw him off that time.'

'Ah yes . . . Stinky.'

'He got into our back garden and hid in the camellia bush. Unfortunately we decided to water the garden with comfrey fertiliser. That's where the terrible smell came from.'

DI Benton's lips quirked, a smile was quickly suppressed.

'I wonder if he'd been lurking in the garden before?' Charlie frowned thoughtfully. 'He must have got this stuff from somewhere and I can't see how else . . . '

DI Benton's expression was serious again. 'Don't play games with me, Charlie. There's only one place he could have got this amount of detail and that's you.' She straightened her back and gave Charlie a level look before she said in a formal tone, 'DC Ainsworth, you have an appointment with the Chief Constable this afternoon at 2.00pm. In the meantime, although someone checked your emails while you were suspended, looking for important ones, there may be others you want to read before you leave. And it's time to tidy your desk.'

'Yes Ma'am.' Charlie knew what this meant. The Chief Constable would be asking for her resignation, a request which would brook no refusal.

Charlie started to tidy her desk and it was all she could do to stave off the tears. This was a job she loved, the only job she'd ever wanted to do, apart from the army — and after Kent's betrayal she didn't think she could face that now because of all the hurtful memories.

Her colleagues treated her with polite aloofness, as if they were afraid to be tainted with her bad behaviour, only conversing when necessary about cases ongoing and closed.

It was all so unfair because she hadn't talked to the press. It must have been the neighbours, she thought. Or perhaps that reporter had bugged them

— though that seemed too fanciful. But how else would he know about the emails? Or maybe it was Mum? Charlie couldn't remember what her mum did and didn't know about the emails.

The hours dragged by until it was lunchtime.

Matt walked into the office looking to spend lunch break with Charlie, but his smile faded when he saw her. 'What's wrong?'

'That rat-bag reporter wrote an 'exclusive' with loads of details he must have scavenged from somewhere. Like I've told you before, coppers can't talk to the press like this. I'm seeing the CC this afternoon and will have to hand in my resignation.'

She couldn't help it; she burst into tears.

Matt turned completely white. 'I thought that was just while things were sub judice. I thought that now Kent's pleaded guilty, talking to the press didn't matter. Where's your boss?'

Matt marched up to DI Benton's

door and knocked hard. Charlie was terrified he was about to do something stupid, so she leapt up and pursued him.

'It was me,' Matt said the second he went in. 'I talked to that gutter reporter. Charlie didn't know anthing about it.'

DI Benton scrutinised Matt's face for about ten seconds, then picked up the phone. 'Hello sir, DI Benton here. Some new information about that newspaper article has come to light, and I think it best if you hear it first hand and immediately. Can we bring the meeting forward to now, please?'

She listened for a couple of minutes, while Charlie and Matt looked on, anxiously silent. 'We'll be right up then, sir.' She put the phone down. 'Now Matt Penningby, not another word until you're in the CC's room. And that goes for you too, Charlie.'

It seemed like a long walk to the CC's office, or perhaps it was just because Charlie's legs didn't seem to be working too well. Matt sought her hand

and squeezed it.

The CC's personal assistant looked up as they arrived. 'Go straight in,' she said.

'Sit down, all of you,' the Chief Constable said. 'Pull up an extra chair, Mr Penningby, I wasn't expecting you. Now, what's this new information?'

'It was me, sir,' said Matt. 'I gave Charlie's story to the reporter, but there were reasons. On Saturday when Charlie was in town getting her hair done I found the reporter in our back garden, sitting at our picnic table having a smoke, cool as a cucumber. We think he was in the garden when the story first broke, hiding in the bushes with his camera.' Matt paused.

'I understand you 'accidentally' watered the garden and him along with it,' said DI Benton.

'And so . . . ?' The Chief Constable prompted Matt to go on.

'I told him to get out of our garden in no uncertain terms, but he refused. I told him he had no right to be there and to shove off, but he just sat there. I told him he was trespassing, and I threatened to call the police, but he said trespass was a civil matter, not a criminal one, and . . . well, I was a bit flummoxed, to tell the truth.'

'You should have phoned,' said Charlie. 'He was just pushing his luck.'

'He said if I touched him he would sue. I asked him what he wanted and he said he wanted an exclusive story. I told him where to stick it but he said he could play it two ways. He told me his camera got damaged when we watered him, and he was going to sue. He said he had enough scraps of information anyway from talking to the neighbours and your dad, Charlie, and what he didn't know he would invent to make a reasonable 'exclusive' and that we could try and sue him if we dared.

'Or, he said, I could give him the exclusive and he'd pay us well for the story. I was terrified he'd sue us and put some really awful things into

Charlie's mouth, if you know what I mean.'

Matt looked down at his own hands in his lap. 'And I have to admit the amount of money he offered was staggering. I made him, or rather his editor, pay up front by credit transfer into my Internet account, and then I shifted it elsewhere.'

Anxiously he turned to look at Charlie. 'I'm sorry Charlie, he'd got me over a barrel and I thought I might as well get something from the wreckage. It's enough to pay back the life insurance, which I know you've been fretting about. I know we haven't found out if you were liable yet or whether Kent should pay it back, but it seemed easier to sort it by paying it off ourselves and it seemed like poetic justice, really. I didn't know it would end like this. I thought I could talk to the papers now it's not sub judice.'

His rambled explanation fizzled out and he look back at his own hands again, shamefaced.

'I've told you before we can't answer back in the press!' Charlie retorted. 'It always goes wrong even if we try. It's part of the job, but it's a job I love — and now you've wrecked it!'

'But I thought it wouldn't matter now . . . not now Kent's just waiting sentence.' Matt made a futile attempt to justify himself.

'How do you think I feel, knowing everyone has read that awful piece? You might have told him things that were true, but the slant of the story is just vicious. It puts me in a bad light — and the service in a bad light.'

'I'm sorry, Charlie, I'm really sorry. I thought it was the best way out of a hole. It was a damage limitation exercise . . . '

'You should have phoned the police — and I bet that was twaddle about the camera.' Charlie barely even registered DI Benton and the Chief Constable, she was so angry. Matt looked utterly crushed. He hid his face in his hands and groaned.

'I see . . . ' the Chief Constable said, pulling everyone's attention towards him. 'And you knew nothing about this exlusive, DC Ainsworth?'

'Not a clue, sir. I would know better than to do a stupid, idiot thing like that.'

She shot a glare across at Matt, who flinched at every word and murmured, 'Sorry . . . '

'Quite,' the Chief Constable. 'I do loathe the gutter press. DC Ainsworth, Mr Penningby, would you wait outside, please?'

Once in the corridor, Matt kept repeating, 'Sorry . . . I'm so sorry . . . ' The look of anguish on his face was too much for Charlie and she relented.

'I know you are, darling,' she sighed. 'You didn't mean for this to happen, but if you'd only asked, I could have told you how this would end. And now the chances are we'll both get the bullet and that really will land us in the brown stuff.'

She drew him into a hug, drawing

comfort from each other, then jumped apart as if doused with water at the sound of a voice from behind.

'Ahem . . . ' The Chief Constable's PA was looking at them with a slightly scandalised expression. 'You can go back in, now.'

They were not invited to sit. The CC and DI Benton were both standing. Here it comes, thought Charlie and braced herself.

'Mr Penningby. I have just spoken to your boss and she tells me your technical work is excellent, and I appreciate the forthright way in which you have told us what happened and why you spoke to the press, but there is no room in my force for someone who shows such a lack of discretion, common sense and resistance to blackmail. I shall expect your resignation on my desk by 15.00.'

'Yes, sir,' said Matt dully.

'Because your technical work is of a very high standard you will still receive good references. I'm sorry, Matt. Learn some sense from this and I wish you luck for the future.' The Chief Constable turned his attention to Charlie. 'DC Ainsworth . . .'

Charlie flinched. 'Sir.'

'I accept that you knew nothing of Mr Penningby speaking to the Press in such an ill-advised way. I have looked at your record and at the reasons behind your recent suspension. It seems to me that you have had a very rough year, and that your husband Kent Henley, whom I understand you to be divorcing, has behaved abominably.

'Having been yourself a victim of fraud, both financial and emotional, you will be able to empathise well with victims. I do have room for you in this force, and DI Benton has room for you in her team . . . but take this as a warning. You need to impress upon Mr Penningby here the need for utter discretion, and you will need to guard your tongue when, and if, you marry him.'

'Yes sir, thank you, sir.' Charlie gave an audible sigh of relief.

14

Matt and Charlie arrived home together early afternoon because DI Benton sent her home with Matt, who had to leave as soon as his resignation was handed in. Matt was very quiet all the way home, not even attempting to say sorry, which was just as well because Charlie was at snapping point. She was both furious with him for being so stupid, and grateful to him for being so honest about it, and saving her job for her.

She was driving, so she could only steal the odd glance at him; his jaw was set tight and he kept swallowing. She longed to hug him, tell him he was forgiven, but part of her was still angry with him, and she was frightened for their future.

As soon as they got in through the front door he fled into the bathroom and she heard the bolt slip across.

Leave him be, she told herself. She put the kettle on, then returned to the door where the post had been ignored. It was mostly junk, and a couple of letters for Matt. She propped them up against a mug she'd primed with instant coffee and sugar in the kitchen. She made her own coffee and went into the living room, put her mug down carefully then flopped into the sofa, leaning back against it with a groan.

It could have been worse, much worse, she thought. At least she still had a job, but how would they manage on one wage?

Matt was taking ages and Charlie began to get worried. She went to the bathroom door and tapped lightly. 'Matt, darling, there's a couple of official-looking letters for you out here.'

The bolt snapped back, the door was flung open and Matt's face, white and blotched red, appeared. He took the letters, glanced briefly at the postmark, opened and read the first with a wince, opened the second, frowned, and put them in his back pocket.

'Anything interesting?' asked Charlie.

'Nope, just junk.'

It hadn't looked like junk mail, but Charlie said nothing and made Matt's coffee. He took it silently and went into the lounge while Charlie started to organise supper. She stuck her head round the lounge door. Matt was on the sofa staring into space. 'Sausages, baked potatoes and salad do you?' she asked, a little too brightly.

'Yeah, whatever.'

Supper was eaten in awkward silence. Matt stood as soon as their cutlery clattered to the plates, and took them through to the kitchen to wash up.

'Let's go for a walk,' suggested Charlie once the drying-up had been done.

'Not for me. You go if you want.'

'Oh, do stop sulking. What's done is done. You'll get another job. It's no good crying over spilt milk.'

'I'm not,' said Matt frostily, 'At least you've still got your job, even if it is a job that treats us like criminals and gets rid of us at the drop of a hat. Well, they can stuff their job!' He stomped into the lounge and put the TV on. 'I only did it for you after all.'

Charlie put her walking shoes on, thinking it was his own damned foolishness that got him into this pickle. But the walk did nothing to abate her anger and frustration, and when she got home, Matt had gone to bed early.

★   ★   ★

The atmosphere was almost as bad next day at work. Everyone was subdued and although they were perfectly polite to her, there was none of the usual chit-chat. Charlie spent the morning orientating herself again and keeping a low profile.

During lunch break she phoned Matt's mobile but got no reply, and when she phoned home she got the answer machine. A sick feeling started to flutter in her stomach. Maybe Matt resented her keeping her job while he had lost his, resented that his honesty had resulted in him being given the boot.

And she'd called him an idiot in front of the Chief Constable, hadn't she? She cringed at the memory and then she remembered the letters he'd read and not shared with her. It reminded her of Kent being so secretive over the credit card bills. Suppose Matt was the same — in debt and too scared to tell her, especially now he had no job.

It's all going horribly wrong, she thought. *Again.*

When she finally got home after a very long and weary day, she asked Matt, 'Anything much in the post?'

'Not a lot,' said Matt in a dull tone. 'I've made supper.'

Charlie waited for him to ask how work had been, but he didn't. She wondered how long she could stand his sulking.

She needed a rant, so she phoned Aunty Sophie and explained what had happened. 'He's driving me nuts with his long, pained silences and his martyred expression,' she concluded. 'I feel for him, Aunty Sophie, but he's wallowing in self-pity and he won't even talk about it.'

'Leave him.' Aunty Sophie's words were calmly decisive.

'I can't do that!' wailed Charlie.

'Silly, I meant leave him *be*, let him sulk. He's had a shock, lost his job, found out that the real world isn't as forgiving as a fairytale one where the hero confesses all nobly. Poor Matt. You're both still very young, you know. He just needs some space. I bet he loved that job.'

'Yes, I think he did. We'd only just gone back to work, too. He was so excited yesterday morning.'

'Well, there you go, then. Girls like to talk things through, men sulk. Best thing is to leave him be. He'll come round.'

* * *

Next day when Charlie got home, Matt yelled from the kitchen, 'Hey — good news! I have an interview!'

'For what?' Charlie joined him. He was grinning widely as he made coffee for them both.

'A job, much better paid than with the police, and good prospects. I hated the way I was being treated and was afraid the suspension would be much longer, so I'd already started job hunting, just out of curiosity at first, then because I decided a couple of weeks ago that I was going to stop working for the police as soon as feasible.'

He gave a chagrined smile. 'I didn't expect the end to come quite so soon, though. Mind you, it's only an interview, and I bet there are loads of candidates. But it's better than the rejections I've been getting.'

'Where is it? And what rejections?' Charlie asked. 'Let's go sit down, I'm shattered.' It was no exaggeration; Charlie felt the same way she did if she lost a night's sleep. The last few days had been so full of emotional tension, and now that she felt a glimmer of hope, she just wanted to sleep.

'I've been applying for jobs for a couple of weeks now, but with no luck. I got two rejections the day I got the bullet. This job's in Pandleford, about half a mile from the Big House, so we could drive in together like before, save on petrol — their car park is less busy than at the Big House.' Matt sipped his coffee. 'This could work out very well, could be a blessing is disguise.'

'Hardly . . . '

'Well, yes,' he countered. 'That crummy reporter's fee paid off the debt so we don't have that to worry about. And if I get this job we can carry on much as before, and we can get married when your divorce is through.'

He put down his mug, picked up her hand and kissed each finger in turn. 'I am sorry, love. I was a heck of a fool but I did mean it for the best. I just couldn't stand to see you so worried about owing the life insurance company, even though it's really Kent's problem. This will give you a clean start. Can you ever forgive me . . . ?'

He turned puppy-dog eyes on her, so full of apologetic appeal she couldn't say what she thought. He'd jeopardised the career she loved so much and the prurient details of their love life had been splashed across the trashiest newspaper in the country.

'That reporter said he was prepared to make it all up. At least this way I got something for it,' he said.

'True,' said Charlie. 'I'm cross, but of course I forgive you. I love you, silly. Tell you what, why don't we go for a walk and a pub meal?'

'Good idea. Especially as the vultures are back.'

'Oh, you are kidding!' Charlie went to the window. Sure enough, there were a couple of reporters outside. She hadn't noticed them on the way in so they must have only just arrived. As she looked, another car drew up. 'It's at times like this I wish we really did have a wasp's nest in the garden. We could stir it up then leave them to it.'

'They wouldn't notice — too thick-skinned.'

Ten minutes later they walked out of the front door and immediately the press were squawking for a story. Charlie noted which way their cars were pointing, and she and Matt started walking in the opposite direction. They heard car engines start up, but once round the corner she led Matt into Sue's garden, the one with a tall Leylandii hedge running along the edge of the property.

'In here and hide. Sue won't mind, I'm sure.' They snuggled into the prickly branches, hiding themselves from casual view.

Matt peeped through to the road. 'There they go. It's like a convoy. What now? Get in the car and go somewhere, or walk round to the Bricklayer's Arms?'

'In the car before they realise we've

shaken them off.'

A window opened and a woman looked out crossly, then laughed. 'Oh, it's you two. What are you doing?'

'Shhh . . . we're hiding from the press. If they ask, can you tell them we've gone to Pandleford?' asked Charlie.

They fled to the car, started up and drove off in a different direction. 'Where shall we go?' she asked. 'I don't fancy anything local because everyone knows us and they'll have read the paper, most likely.'

Matt cringed slightly, guilty conscience obviously giving him grief. 'There's a good pub near Kindleby that my parents used to go to. I haven't been for years. It's in the middle of some lovely woods, even nicer than the bluebell woods near here.'

Charlie kept looking in the mirror for a tail. This is getting *ridiculous*, she thought; nobody was following them.

They parked in the pub car park, booked a table for eight o'clock, then went for a walk. It was a lovely evening, the woods cool and sheltered, the air fresh. Charlie wove her fingers between Matt's and they walked along, pace for pace just like years ago.

As if he was reading her thoughts Matt said, 'We ought to start hill walking again. I used to enjoy going youth hostelling when we were kids.'

'Good idea. I could do with getting fit.' She glanced at Matt. He had a bounce in his step again, and a faint quirk to his lips. He'd just been required to resign after an emotionally gruelling few months, and might not get this job, but an interview was an interview and if he was attractive to one employer, he would surely be attractive to others until he found something.

He deserved to be a little bit hopeful after being so horrified and contrite. She tried to imagine how Kent would have behaved under the same circumstances, but she really couldn't guess.

'How long do you think he'll get?' asked Matt. It was amazing how they seemed to be thinking of the same things at the same time, as if they were talking by telepathy.

'I don't know. They'll take his guilty pleas into account, and maybe his circumstances — that's what they're after when they ask for pre-sentence reports. I really don't know.

'But they're serious charges, Matt, and Military Court is very strict. He was AWOL for so long it's viewed as desertion. He'll be booted out of his regiment, that's for sure.

'But let's not talk about him. I want this evening to be about us — our future.'

With every step Charlie felt her own shoulder muscles unknotting. She hadn't realised how tense she was.

15

'How did the interview go?' asked Charlie as she walked in through the front door. 'I got Chinese on the way home. I fancied a change.' Actually she'd got Chinese because she knew how much Matt loved it, and she'd got his favourite dishes to either celebrate or console, depending on the circumstances. Her heart thudded painfully as she waited for his reply, knowing how much good news would mean to him.

Matt came out of the living room with a wary grin on his face, grabbed her, kissed her, then took the takeaway from her.

'Love you. I'm starved. It went okay, I suppose. Hard to tell really. It was gruelling, though. And there was a practical session as well, which was rather sprung on us, though I did fine with that. And then I had to answer the thorny question about why I'd resigned . . . I said I felt uncomfortable with the way we'd been treated and felt it was time for a change.

'I had to tell them about the suspension and everything — I thought it would be better to be up front . . . I hope my references are good — they did promise.' He pulled a couple of plates from the cupboard and started to serve up the meal. 'I am ravenous.'

'Me too.' Charlie wondered whether to open a bottle of wine, but decided against it in case it seemed like tempting fate.

Matt looked happier than he had for days, weeks even. The thought frightened her because she wondered how he would feel if he didn't get the job. Maybe he'd be all moody and unbearable again, maybe he'd decide she wasn't worth the angst. She quelled a feeling of panic, took their plates over to the kitchen table and sat down.

'Something else, love,' Matt told her. 'It looks as if your decree nisi is through. You could be free in six weeks. The letter's on the mantelpiece. I'll go get it.'

He handed her the envelope, which she opened carefully and scanned the contents. 'Thank Goodness. Six weeks minimum. Let's hope they don't drag their heels.'

Just then, the phone went, making her jump.

They exchanged a concerned glance before Matt grabbed it.

'Yes, speaking . . . ' His eyes lit up as he went on, 'Oh that's excellent! Yes, yes, I can start straight away. That's fine. Thanks! Goodbye.'

He turned to Charlie. 'My old boss emailed the references through and they must have been good. I start tomorrow — though I'm on six months' probation.'

Charlie stood up and flung herself into his arms and he gave her a deep, loving kiss as she melted into his body.

'Well done you,' she told him. 'I wish we had some bubbly to celebrate, but we'll have to make do with plonk.'

She pulled out the white wine that was chilling in the fridge, unscrewed the cap and poured two generous measures into the glasses Matt pulled from the cupboard.

'Here's to the future.'

'Here's to our future,' agreed Matt. 'Now let's eat!'

★   ★   ★

Charlie waited in the Big House car park for Matt to come and pick her up. He drove up and she jumped in and belted up. 'Well, how was your first day?'

'I'm shattered. Information overload. But it's great,' Matt grinned. 'The people are really cool, the job is challenging enough to be interesting without being stressful and the work space is nice and new.'

'Great. Let's stop off and buy some bubbly, and maybe something special for supper.'

Matt couldn't stop talking all the way home. He scooped up the post as they went in through the front door, while Charlie carried the shopping in. He sifted the junk post straight into the recycling bin, then frowned over one envelope.

'Here's one for you . . . the writing seems familiar.'

Charlie took it, turned it over a couple of times; she recognised the writing at once, though she said nothing.

Kent. Her impulse was to throw it away unread, or to read it later when Matt wasn't around, but looking at his suddenly anxious face she knew she had to open it there and then, and share whatever the contents were.

The longer she left it, the more afraid she was to open the envelope, so she took a deep breath and tugged at it, hands trembling. Pulling out a sheaf of paper, she scanned through to the end. 'It's from Kent,' she told Matt and started to read it aloud to him.

My darling Charlie . . .

'That's a cheek, for a start!' she said. 'I'm no darling of his. Not now anyway.'

Soon our divorce will be through and now that I've been sentenced and know what the next few years will bring, I would like to see you one last time. I was disappointed you didn't come to see me sentenced. I thought you could have been that kind at least in memory of the love we had and that I still have for you. I know I've done wrong but it's because I love you, always have. I'm sorry for what I did, it was all because of PTSD, Post Traumatic Stress Disorder in case you don't know, it made me do things I wouldn't dream of normally. I've been getting treatment for it in The Glasshouse, but now my sentence is through I've been discharged from the army and have been transferred to HM Prison Pandleford. I want you

*to come and see me so I can explain
and say sorry and I want you to do
this soon, before the decree nisi is
through. I want to say sorry to you
while we're still man and wife. I
expect you know how to come and
see me.*

*Love
Kent.*

'Don't go,' Matt said straight away.
'He's only trying to twist you round, he
wants you to stop the divorce.'

'Not a chance. But I suppose I had
better go and see him.'

'What? You just said no chance.'

'I meant no chance of stopping the
divorce, but I think I should go and see
him. I owe him that much.'

'But why? You owe him nothing. He's
behaved abominably.'

'He was ill, mentally wounded. If he
hadn't got Post Traumatic Stress
Disorder he wouldn't have behaved like
that.'

'You reckon? He's a swindler, always

has been. All's fair in love and war — his phrase. I remember him saying that when we were cadets together doing exercises. He'd cheat then, and call it using his initiative. We thought it was funny at the time, but now we're older we can see it for what it was. I think he's using the stress as an excuse. I bet he never had it.'

'Yes, he did, he does . . . you never saw him after he came back from Iraq. He was different. He'd wake up in the night, terrified. You don't know what it's like if you've never had it.'

'And you have, I suppose.'

'Don't think so, though some of the things I saw on Response could turn anyone's head. But I saw how Kent was, and he was ill. He'd promised to see someone about it after he came back from Phuket. But by that time it was too late.'

'You're not to go. I don't trust him.' Matt stuck his jaw out.

'How dare you dictate to me what I must and must not do!'

'You still love him.'

'Oh, don't be so silly!'

'You must do or you wouldn't want to go and see him. You took ages to decide for us to become lovers and now I know why — you were still in love with him.'

'But I thought we'd decided . . . You were the one who said you didn't want to catch me on the rebound, or take advantage of me while I was still vulnerable — you were the one who wanted to wait until a decent amount of time had passed.'

Matt merely shrugged, knowing it was the truth.

'We decided this together, discussed it, decided at first to hold off until we could get married, but then we decided not to wait when we found that Trevor was missing and I might not be free to marry you for ages,' Charlie reminded him. 'So I can't understand the fuss. We made those decisions together, rationally. I'm yours, and yours alone, now. I don't still love him.'

'Don't go then,' Matt said through gritted teeth.

'I refuse to discuss this while you're being so pigheaded.' Charlie unlocked the back door, went into the garden, and watered the plants with the hose, her thoughts tumbling over themselves as her heart rate dropped back to normal.

He's just jealous, she told herself. *He's feeling vulnerable and he's not thinking straight. Kent's a prize rat and no way would I stop the divorce. But Matt is remembering back to when we were kids and easily manipulated . . .*

Suddenly, Charlie felt a sense of shock.

Kent had manipulated them both even when they were kids, and she'd only just realised it!

She turned the hose off and went back indoors, but the kitchen was empty. The letter was on the side where she'd left it, but looked as if it had been thrown in the bin then retrieved because it was stained in one corner.

She read it through again and was still undecided.

It seemed like a mixture of contrition and need, with an icing of selfishness. Typically Kent.

But perhaps this was his way of trying to say sorry. Still, she didn't need to make any decisions yet. She shoved the letter in her handbag and threw the envelope in the recycling bin.

She filled the kettle, then yelled, 'Do you want a cup of tea?'

Matt didn't reply; he was probably sulking. She knew better now than to go in search of him just yet, so she made a pot of tea and unpacked the shopping before going upstairs with a cup.

She knocked on the door. 'I've brought you a cuppa.' No reply. She pushed the handle down, peeped round the edge of the door. The room was empty.

The house was empty, his car was gone.

★ ★ ★

Charlie sent a text: *I love you, pls come home.*

Throughout the evening she wavered between anger and fear. He was being foolish, and how dare he try to manipulate her like this, make her feel guilty? But supposing that was it — what if he'd had enough, decided he didn't love her after all?

Suppose he'd gone to do something stupid? But she reminded herself that he wasn't like that.

Where could he have gone, though?

He had to be at work the next day. Surely he wouldn't chuck in his new job just because they'd had a silly row?

And as for throwing that special decision back in her face; that was unkind — and unnecessary considering they were now lovers — even hypocritical since it had been partly his idea to behave honourably while she was still in shock. What had he to be jealous about?

She sent a couple more texts. Both went unanswered.

At midnight she finally went to bed,

although she couldn't sleep, listening out for the front door.

* * *

Next morning she popped her head round the spare bedroom door. He hadn't sneaked in and slept there. She went downstairs, looked out the front door. His car wasn't there. She showered, drank a cup of tea, but couldn't face breakfast.

She left a note on the kitchen table: *I love you.*

When Charlie arrived at work, as soon as DI Benton saw her face, she said. 'I think you and I need a talk in my office . . . with coffee. A good strong one by the looks of it.'

When they were seated with a coffee, which Charlie sipped gratefully, DI Benton said, 'So tell me what's up then?'

Charlie found it impossible to answer, so she fished out Kent's letter and handed it to DI Benton, who read it with lips

297

compressing harder with each line.

'You don't have to go and see him, you know. And sorry, I suppose it would have been a courtesy to tell you when he was due to be sentenced but other things got in the way of that.'

Other things being a trashy newspaper article and Matt's resignation, presumably.

'It's not just that, ma'am . . . Matt and I had a row over it.' Charlie recounted what had happened, finishing up with, 'He was being so unreasonable.'

'And when was any row ever reasonable?' asked DI Benton. 'A reasonable row is a debate or a discussion, not a row.'

She sighed and gave Charlie a long look before asking, 'How do you feel about all of this? I mean, do you want to go and see Kent, despite Matt's jealousy? And how do you feel about Matt's sulking forcing your hand? If you ask me both men are trying to manipulate you, though I do have some sympathy with Matt's position. Not Kent, though, he deserves all he got — and he doesn't deserve you, and you know that,' she said firmly.

'I don't really want to see Kent, to be honest, but I think I might, for the sake of closure and to make sure he knows I never want to speak to him again.'

Charlie stared into her coffee and added, 'As for Matt, you're right, he is having a tantrum, and if I give in over this, I'll end up giving in over every disagreement if he has a tantrum.'

'Give in to toddlers and they wind you round their little finger.'

'But I'm frightened that he won't come back. I'm worried our relationship has fallen apart before it's ever really got going.'

'If it falls apart this easily then perhaps it's better if it ends now. Matt needs to grow up a bit, needs to understand that not everything is black and white, that there are nuances, and that your love for him is strong. He needs to learn to trust you. It sounds to me like he's frightened of losing you, and is pushing you away so that he doesn't get hurt.'

'That doesn't make sense.'

'No, it doesn't, but think about what Kent did with those emails, very successfully splitting you both, and then Kent wooed you and married you.'

'Wooed!' Charlie burst out laughing.

'Just because a word is old fashioned . . . ' said DI Benton with a staged haughty sniff.

'Suppose Matt hasn't gone to work? I'm frightened he might have done something stupid.'

'If he's skived off work, he's a fool, but I doubt he'll have done anything stupid. Maybe he's gone to a mate's house overnight. His parents live some way away now, don't they?'

Charlie nodded. 'I haven't a clue where to look and, bother it, why should I go running around after him?' She chewed her lip. 'And no way did I want to phone his parents.'

'You know what I would do?' DI

Benton suggested. 'I would see if you can spot his car in his new company's car park, then if it's there, phone the switchboard and ask to speak to him. Just tell him he's an idiot — no, tell him you love him. And do it now, because I can't see you concentrating on your work until it's done. You'll have to work late to make up for it, though.'

Matt's car was in the car park. Charlie drove back to the Big House, then phoned his works switchboard, asked to be put through. 'Matt Penningby speaking. How can I help?'

'By coming home tonight and giving me a hug.'

'Charlie darling, I'm sorry, I went to cool off and the longer I left it, the sillier I felt until I didn't dare come home. I thought you didn't love me — how can you bear to go and see him after all he's done if you don't love him?'

'You idiot, of course I love you. I always have.'

'I can't talk now, I'll see you later.'

'I might have to work late, so don't panic if I'm not there,' added Charlie quickly.

'Okay, love you.'

Charlie closed her phone up, then allowed a relieved smile to spread across her face.

★ ★ ★

When she got home that night she was overjoyed to see Matt's car already there. She opened the front door tentatively and Matt came out of the kitchen, giving her an abashed smile. 'I've been getting supper ready ... what we didn't eat last night. Forgive me? I won't hug you because my hands are all oniony.'

Charlie walked up to him, kissing him. 'Of course I forgive you, though please don't ever do that to me again. I was worried and angry at the same time, and I'm really tired as I didn't sleep very well. Where were you?'

'I didn't sleep well either. I slept in

my car and it's not comfy. Then I went and had a burger and coffee, had a shave in a disabled loo, then went to work. I feel a bit shabby.'

Charlie filled the kettle. 'I think an early night would be sensible. I'm starved — and shattered.'

'What have you decided to do about Kent?'

'I haven't decided anything yet. But whatever I do decide, I love you, not him, want to spend the rest of my life with you, and nothing he could say would ever change my mind . . . actually, let's not talk about it tonight, love I don't see why his stupid, selfish letter should cause us any more grief.'

'You're right, 'nuff said.'

Matt washed his hands then gave her a proper hug, one that warmed her to her toes.

★ ★ ★

Kent was a taboo subject and Charlie tried not to think about him. The days slid by and the row receded into the past. And then another letter from Kent arrived, begging her to see him.

'Tell him to get knotted,' said Matt. 'You could write to him.' They were sitting entwined on the sofa.

'I could. I wonder why he wants to see me before the decree nisi?' Charlie looked into the middle distance.

'I think he wants to change your mind.'

'Then he's a fool. Let's draft a reply together.'

'What was his sentence, do you know?' Matt asked. 'I mean, did DI Benton tell you?'

'I don't know. Nobody told me, and she didn't when we had our little heart to heart.'

'What heart-to-heart?'

'The day after our row when you didn't come home; she took one look at me and called me in for a chat.'

'Oh.' A faint redness crept up Matt's neck, then he stood and fetched his laptop. 'I wonder if it was reported anywhere. I would have expected it to be, after all the hounding we've had to put up with.'

'Well, if it was, we missed it. I think the local paper puts headlines online in the hopes you'll buy the paper.'

Matt put Kent's name into a search engine. 'Found something. He was sentenced to six years for the frauds and two for desertion; that's to be served concurrently.' Matt looked at her with a bleak expression. 'When we were kids I thought we'd be pals forever. I thought we'd all three join the army. I never expected it to end like this.'

'Me neither . . . I bet he didn't, either.' Charlie snuggled in closer to Matt. 'It was all right until we started to grow up. It's kind of why I'm torn about going to see him. I feel like it'll never be over until I tell him face to face how he's hurt me and why I never want to see him again . . . but, Matt, I'm scared.'

'Don't go, then,' he said. 'You know you don't have to.'

'But I'm scared not to. He could be out in three years on licence. I don't want him to spend those three years in hope, thinking that there's a connection between us.'

'So let's write that letter, then, and tell him.'

Several drafts on the computer, and numerous cups of coffee later, Charlie was finally satisfied with the letter . . .

Kent,

I see no reason to come and see you, particularly before the decree nisi is through. Marrying you was my biggest mistake. I thought I loved you, and meant my vows at the time, but the person I thought I was marrying died the day I found out it was you who sent that email to Matt supposedly from me, splitting us up. If you hadn't done that I might have married Matt years ago, and things would have been very different. You might have found someone else, you and Trev would never have gone to

Phuket and Trev would still be alive and you would not be where you are now.

But once on that path, you chose to continue; making me responsible for your debts, taking Trev's place and selling his home, and worst of all was the hell I went through when I thought you were dead. You broke my heart — and when I found out how despicable you'd been, you broke it again.

You came back from Iraq a changed man. Perhaps if you'd done something about it then, we could have had a good life together — but then again, perhaps you would have simply pulled us both into debt.

In many ways what's happened is poetic justice. I would never have found out about those despicable emails if we had not needed to contact your friends with the sad news of your 'death'. If you had come home and told us the truth about Trev, then I would have been none the wiser.

If you hope for a reconciliation you are sadly misguided. I never want to see you again. You have caused me and all your friends and family such pain and grief.

I hope you get over your problems. Perhaps prison will change you for the better and when you get out I hope you find the right woman — but that woman is not me. Matt and I will get married as soon as we can. We were destined for each other until you interfered.

Charlie.

Charlie read it through, then found herself in tears. Matt saved the text, put the laptop down, hugged and rocked her. 'Oh, my darling, my love, don't cry. It'll all be over soon, and we can get married and put this behind us.'

The next morning Charlie read through it one last time, printed it off, and sent it.

$\star \quad \star \quad \star$

Four days later she got another letter from Kent that was starkly to the point.

Charlie,
Please come and see me, I beg you. I'm not going to try to make you change your mind, I just want to see you. Bring Matt if you want. Please. I need to see you one last time.
Kent

Charlie took the mug of coffee that Matt handed to her. '*I want, I need . . .* that's just so typical,' she said. 'He's still trying to manipulate.' She sipped her coffee, looking into the distance.

Matt gently took the letter from her. 'Perhaps we should go. Can we go together . . . is that allowed?'

'I don't know. I'm a bit loath when all the other inmates will be being visited by their wives . . . actually . . . ' She fell silent, thinking. 'I wonder if we can arrange a special visit where the others won't see us visiting him . . . ? There might be some old lags in there because of my testimony, you see, and if I'm recognised as a copper it could lead to trouble. Much though I despise Kent for what he's done, I wouldn't want him to end up with trouble while he's inside.'

16

Charlie quickly rubbed her hands on her trousers and tried to get her heart rate under control. This was worse, far worse than walking to the witness box. Matt gave her what he obviously thought was a reassuring smile, but it looked like a grimace.

They submitted to being searched, then were ushered to what reminded Charlie of an interview room, and invited to sit. Then Kent was brought in, supervised by a prison officer. Kent looked for a minute as if he expected Charlie to jump up and kiss him, and when she didn't he sat at the table opposite them.

'Thanks for coming,' he said quietly.

Charlie thought that in a strange way he looked better than he had for a long time, more like the Kent she used to know before he joined the army. He looked lighter, and bizarrely under the circumstances, freer.

Perhaps Kent hadn't been suited to the army after all. They'd all told each other that's what they would do, but Kent was the only one who had. She tried to imagine Matt with a gun, killing people, or herself shooting someone. She couldn't see it, really couldn't see it. Maybe Kent should never have joined up either.

Kent's voice broke her reveries. 'I've been wanting to say I'm sorry for a long time . . . ' he began haltingly. 'Look, I know this wasn't what you wanted, but please . . . I need to explain. Then you go your way, I'll go mine . . . or rather, I'll go mine when I get out of here.' A ghost of as smile crossed his lips.

'I've done some awful things, I know that, but I never meant any harm. But once things started to go wrong, they just kept on getting worse. You were right, the email was the first wrong thing I did, and it just got worse from there. I was jealous of Matt because I could see you were falling for him, and I was — I still am — in love with you.'

Kent shifted awkwardly in his seat. 'So I set up the spoof email account and Matt fell for it. I suppose I didn't expect it to be so easy, I expected it to be found out, for you to phone each other, to get back together . . . if you'd sussed it was me that sent it I would have passed it off as a joke, I suppose. But truly, I only did it because I love you, Charlie, and I wanted you.'

Kent turned to Matt. 'Sorry mate, I really thought at the time that all's fair in love and war . . . my dad used to say that, you know . . . I was wrong, but at the time I was chuffed because you went off to university and me and Charlie carried on the same.

'I suppose I should have guessed we weren't right for each other when she kept turning me down for one reason or another.

'And then we went to Iraq.' Kent fell silent for a few moments then said, 'Did Charlie tell you about Simbo?'

'A bit, though not much, just that some mates died, including your best mate Simbo, and you came back changed. Post Traumatic Stress or something. Did you tell them? In your court martial, I mean?'

'Yeah, they knew. But the thing is, it's well known nowadays, and if we think we're affected, we're supposed to go sick, not AWOL. It counts against us if we don't seek help. And I didn't.'

Charlie bit her lip, wondering if perhaps she should have done more to help Kent, insisted he saw someone sooner, rather than leave it so late — even spoken to his CO.

'Even so I would never have gone AWOL if the tsunami hadn't happened. It was an impulse,' Kent added.

'So what really happened?' asked Matt.

'We'd been having a good time, but I was feeling a bit under the weather and was upstairs in the hotel room. Trev was by the pool chatting up some talent when the wave struck . . . I don't remember much, though sometimes I get nightmares still . . . and I felt like I was cursed with bad luck and all my mates were dying around me. I felt so guilty, like it was my fault.'

Charlie reached out and touched Kent's hand. Matt glanced at her, then reached out and laid his own on Kent's other hand.

Kent gave a shuddering sigh. 'Trev was easy to identify but on the spur of the moment I said he was me. Just like that. On impulse. No thought, nothing, just said it. But then there was no going back.

'It wasn't until I'd done it that I thought of all the other stuff . . . I knew Trev was an orphan, only child . . . he was pretty well off, owned his house outright after his parents died in an accident. That's when he left the army, so there were no complications. I knew I was insured and thought you'd be raking it in, Charlie. I reckoned you'd only need about half of it to pay the debts.'

'Well, you thought wrong,' Charlie levelled an accusing stare at him, angry again. 'I did use half of it for your debts but I only got half because you weren't officially dead. The coroner wanted Trev's testimony, but Trev had vanished and you sold his house.'

'I had to — his neighbours knew him.'

'How the heck did you rack up so much debt in the first place, Kent?' Charlie asked.

He shrugged. 'I wanted a nice car to impress you and the insurance cost a packet. So I bought everything else on credit cards, and started juggling the money. It was too easy — but then it got out of hand.'

'But you forged my signature on the credit card agreement. That made me a suspect when you reappeared.'

'I had to. Like I said, things were getting out of hand and I needed to buy your Christmas pressie — and the holiday and stuff.'

Charlie gave him an aghast look, then

shook her head.

'Charlie was beside herself with worry on Boxing Day,' Matt said accusingly. 'And your family were bereft, yet you still carried on with the scam. I saw their grief, Kent . . . it was awful.'

Kent withdrew his hands from under theirs, rested his elbows on the table and hid his face in his hands.

'I thought you loved me. It was a funny way of showing it.'

'Oh, Charlie, it was like I was still in the tsunami, washed here and there, out of control,' Kent lamented. 'Once I said the body was me not Trev, that was it, I wasn't in control any more. I . . . I was going to come back to you. I thought you'd be pleased to see me . . . keep my secret, let me lead my life as Trev . . . I thought you loved me, so I went to your house, rang the bell, and then . . . ' Kent shook his head.

'What about Trev's friends? His family? In assuming his identity you prevented them from mourning him properly. They've only now been told it was Trev who died, not you — how must that have been for them?' Charlie wailed. 'It was bad enough how upset and confused I was when 'Trev' didn't come to tell me what had happened. I would have expected my husband's best mate to have the decency to come and tell me how he died.'

'I couldn't, could I? Not without giving the game away. And Trev didn't have any family.'

'He has an aunt, an uncle, cousins . . . you stole their inheritance from them when you sold his house.'

Kent looked up. 'I didn't know.'

'What the heck did you spend it all on?' asked Matt.

'I didn't. Most of it's buried in an ammo box in our old camp on Honeyhook Hill. That's why I needed to talk to you, Charlie; to make sure you're all right. I could have left it there while I'm inside, but I thought you deserved it after the debt I left you in. Use it, Charlie. Pay your mortgage off with it. I don't need it. I want a completely clean start when I get out of here.'

'It's not mine, Kent, it's Trev's; it belongs to Trev's family. You really are impossible. What an utterly selfish thing to do.'

'Hey, come on . . . I didn't know about them. I just wanted to see you and Matt right after all the trouble I caused.'

Charlie wondered if he was lying still, but perhaps he wasn't. Perhaps this was his clumsy ill-thought-out way of wishing them well. 'I'll have to tell my boss, get it sorted officially.'

'If that's what you want, then do it. But just think, Charlie. It could solve a lot of problems.'

'And cause a whole load more, including making a criminal of me. Oh, Kent, you have a lot to learn. I can't believe . . . '

'All right, all right, I'm sorry. Do you forgive me?'

'I really don't know,' said Charlie

slowly. 'But I do understand a lot better now, and that's a weight off my mind.'

'And mine,' said Matt.

'Time's up. Time to say goodbye now,' the prison officer told them all.

Kent nodded. 'Okay then. Thanks for coming. So this is it, then, this is goodbye . . . '

'It is, Kent,' Charlie said firmly. 'Please don't write, don't come and see us after you get out. It will only cause more harm and heartbreak. You get better, get out, and make your own life from now on.'

'I promise,' said Kent softly.

Charlie thought that perhaps he really meant it this time.

When they got in the car Charlie thought she saw tears gleaming in Matt's eyes, but that could have been her own.

'You were right. I'm glad we went after all,' murmured Matt. 'I feel we can all move on now.'

17

The Registry Office didn't have the glamour of a church wedding. Charlie allowed herself to think back to the day of her wedding to Kent; a big white wedding, complete with all the trimmings. And yet there was none of the doubt, none of the cold feet she had felt on that other day. It all felt so long ago now; so much had happened between now and then.

Today was very much a quiet, private affair; just family and a few special friends, which was the way both she and Matt wanted it. They had both had enough of the limelight for several lifetimes over these last few months.

Among their guests were DI Kaye Benton and Richard Benton of course. Despite all that had happened Charlie thought of Kaye as one of her best friends. There had been several times when Kaye in both her guises had saved Charlie from making more of a muddle of things than she already had. She knew she would be disciplined in an instant by DI Benton if she made a fool of herself, but she also knew Kaye Benton would do what she could to prevent her doing so in the first place.

There was less pomp and ceremony at the Registry Office, but much less pressure, too — although Charlie knew she was taking the right decision this time and had no cold feet at all.

She took her vows and looked into the eyes of the man she loved. His hair had flopped forward in that boyishly endearing way she loved so much, and she brushed it back as he bent to kiss her; a chaste brush of the lips.

'Later,' he whispered softly and she felt dizzy at the thought.

They held the small reception at their own house, the guests casually spilling out into the garden to enjoy the last of the late summer sunshine.

At the posh reception after her

wedding with Kent, she'd felt like an actress, like she was just playing a part. But now, with Matt, she felt real. This was real; her love for Matt was real.

It was so easy for her now to imagine them in fifty, sixty, seventy years' time, their hair rimed with frost, and still loving each other in the same way.

Charlie sat on the hammock next to Matt and they swung gently, enjoying the company of their friends. The party lasted well into the night and Matt and Charlie weren't going on honeymoon — were in no hurry to go anywhere.

Why would they be? They had their own home, their beloved garden — and, most importantly, they had each other.

THE END

We do hope that you have enjoyed reading this large print book.

Did you know that all of our titles are available for purchase?

We publish a wide range of high quality large print books including:
Romances, Mysteries, Classics
General Fiction
Non Fiction and Westerns

Special interest titles available in large print are:
The Little Oxford Dictionary
Music Book, Song Book
Hymn Book, Service Book

Also available from us courtesy of Oxford University Press:
Young Readers' Dictionary
(large print edition)
Young Readers' Thesaurus
(large print edition)

For further information or a free brochure, please contact us at:
Ulverscroft Large Print Books Ltd.,
The Green, Bradgate Road, Anstey,
Leicester, LE7 7FU, England.
Tel: (00 44) **0116 236 4325**
Fax: (00 44) **0116 234 0205**

CONFLICT OF HEARTS

Liz Fielding

Lizzie was astounded when her widowed father decided to marry Noah Jordan's beautiful sister. Thinking that now was the time to find a husband of her own — she wasn't about to accept Noah's marriage proposal . . . Noah was rich, gorgeous, charming, but to him marriage to Lizzie was a means of keeping her under control — a temporary measure to give the newly-weds time alone. But Lizzie, determined not to become a convenient bride, faced Noah — who was equally determined to have her!

MY SECRET LOVE

Margaret Mounsdon

When Tamara Cameron's modelling career is cut short after she suffers an injury to her back, she runs a private catering business, relieved to be out of the media spotlight at a time of personal difficulty. But then, scatty Phyllis Morton appears on her doorstep and Tamara's life begins to lurch from one crisis to another, as Phyllis turns out to be the great aunt of Adam Penrose — a man whose marriage proposal she turned down years ago.

KEEPING SECRETS

Della Galton

Twenty-two years ago, Joanna gave up her baby girl for adoption, but she has never forgotten her. When Caroline comes back into her life Joanna is both thrilled and afraid: her son, Robbie, doesn't know about Caroline's existence, and Joanna's marriage to Mike is in crisis. Her long lost daughter couldn't have arrived at a more turbulent moment. Only time will tell if Caroline's presence will reunite the family or destroy it altogether . . .